W9-BNM-483

The Contagious Colors of
Mumpley Middle School

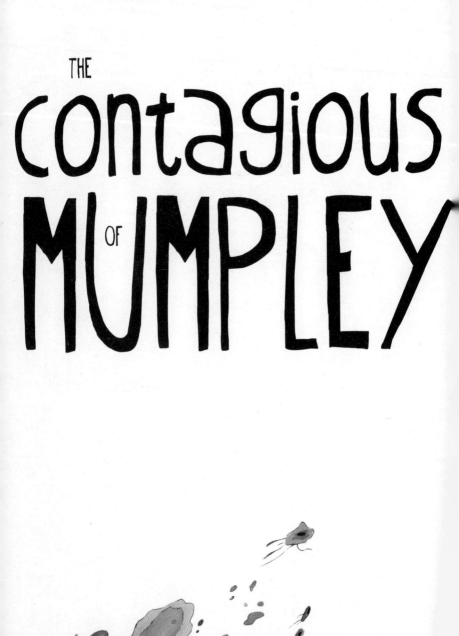

COLORS
middle
SCHOOL

by FOWLER DEWITT

illustrated by
RODOLFO MONTALVO

ATHENEUM BOOKS FOR YOUNG READERS · New York   London   Toronto   Sydney   New Delhi

$\mathcal{A}$
atheneum

ATHENEUM BOOKS FOR YOUNG READERS
An imprint of Simon & Schuster Children's Publishing Division
1230 Avenue of the Americas, New York, New York 10020
This book is a work of fiction. Any references to historical events, real people, or real places are used fictitiously. Other names, characters, places, and events are products of the author's imagination, and any resemblance to actual events or places or persons, living or dead, is entirely coincidental.
For information about special discounts for bulk purchases, please contact Simon & Schuster Special Sales at 1-866-506-1949 or business@simonandschuster.com.
The Simon & Schuster Speakers Bureau can bring authors to your live event. For more information or to book an event, contact the Simon & Schuster Speakers Bureau at 1-866-248-3049 or visit our website at www.simonspeakers.com.
Book design by Lauren Rille
The text for this book is set in Excelsior.
The illustrations for this book are rendered in pen and ink, brush, and digital color.
Manufactured in the United States of America
0813 FFG
First Edition
10 9 8 7 6 5 4 3 2 1
Library of Congress Cataloging-in-Publication Data
DeWitt, Fowler.
The contagious colors of Mumpley Middle School / Fowler DeWitt ; illustrated by Rodolfo Montalvo. — 1st ed.
p.   cm.
Summary: When a mysterious illness sweeps through school, causing students to change color, sixth-grader scientist Wilmer Dooley tries to find the cause and cure.
ISBN 978-1-4424-7829-9 (hardcover)
ISBN 978-1-4424-7831-2 (eBook)
[1. Science—Methodology—Fiction. 2. Diseases—Fiction. 3. Middle schools—Fiction. 4. Schools—Fiction.] I. Montalvo, Rodolfo, ill. II. Title.
PZ7.D526Co 2013
[Fic]—dc23   2012043783

To my long-lost Caroline.
I should have packed the parachute more carefully.
-F. D.

To my parents, Rodolfo Sr. and Cecilia Montalvo,
for all their courage and sacrifice,
and to my wife, René,
for giving me the greatest start I could have ever hoped for.
-R. M.

WEDNESDAY
Day 2

Dear Journal,

Black widow spiders are horrible creatures. Not only do they have a deadly, venomous bite, but the females eat their mates. The girl spider spins the guy tightly in her webbing so he can't move. And then she chews him up.

That's where the name black widow comes from. A widow is a lady whose husband is dead. Or in this case, swallowed whole.

I'm glad I'm not a spider.

Still, who knows what sixth-grade girls are capable of doing to us guys? After all, I've never had any sort of romantic pursuit before. This is unproven scientific ground for me. But I'll take my chances with Roxie. She doesn't seem like the guy-eating sort.

Which means I'll continue my trial-and-error approach, for now at least. Unfortunately, that approach has been all error so far.

Scientific note: When swiping flowers from the school flower bed, check closely for bees.

But when you run into a dead end, it's best to reexamine the facts. Sometimes a quick summary helps form a sound, scientific conclusion.

What do we know about the test subject?

- Roxie McGhee is the most fantastically glorious girl in the sixth grade.
- She is the star reporter of the school paper, MUMPLEY MUSINGS. And her school-broadcast radio show is heavenly.
- She smells like rosebuds blooming on a dewy morning. (Really. My examinations of dewy rosebuds show an 86.3 percent similarity with Roxie's aroma, based on a sample of hair I plucked last week. Or maybe the rosebud scent came from her shampoo. I will need to test further.)

I'll need a new plan to get her to notice me. They say you can't bake a cake without breaking a few eggs! That is, unless you heat the eggshells to 825 degrees Celsius and melt them, like Mom's ill-fated scrambled eggshell omelet disaster last month.

But it wouldn't be science if you didn't have a few unexpected pitfalls along the way, whether from love or from egg yolks burning through the stove top. That's why we have fire extinguishers.

Signing off,
Wilmer Dooley

I.

Wilmer closed his journal and stared one row up and three seats over. That's where Roxie McGhee sat, sandwiched between her best friends, Vonda Binkowski and Claire Huddleston. Like Roxie, Vonda and Claire had long, flowing blond hair and gleaming white teeth. They usually wore matching skirts and long socks. But Claire and Vonda weren't

Roxie. Their cheeks didn't form small dimples when they smiled. Their blue eyes (Wilmer preferred to think of them as low-melanin-pigmented eyes) didn't glitter when they laughed. Wilmer imagined swapping seats with Vonda or Claire. He would lean over to Roxie and say something witty. She would say she loved flowers and not to worry about the bee sting on her arm.

But Wilmer hadn't the nerve. So he stayed where he sat, butt firmly planted behind his desk in the corner of the last row.

The last row was the best place for observation. Back there he could watch everyone in class, away from prying eyes.

Science was all about observation, and Wilmer prided himself on his scientific talents. He was the best student scientist in all of Mumpley Middle School. Despite what Claudius Dill believed.

"We will be doing our final project of the year on medieval diseases," said Mr. Havendash, the history teacher. He was a short man with a long beard, which he liked to stroke as he talked. "In medieval times all sorts of horrible diseases spread unchecked, like leprosy and scurvy. But the most dreaded of all diseases was the bubonic plague, also known as the Black Death. The bubonic plague wiped out somewhere between 30 and 40 percent of the entire population of Europe. We're talking hundreds of millions of people. Imagine if a disease like that struck us today!"

Wilmer sat in his seat, half listening to the teacher. Roxie brushed back her hair and smiled, a smile so bright and warm that Wilmer supposed it could generate enough electricity to light up half the town of Mumpley.

Roxie glanced sideways and spied Wilmer staring at her. Embarrassed, Wilmer quickly looked down at his feet. Did Roxie blush? Her face turned pink, a very bright pink—more like an abnormally vibrant fuchsia, to be exact. But Wilmer wasn't sure, and he didn't dare look up, in case she caught him spying. Again. He continued to stare at his feet.

His shoe was untied. Which meant a 14 percent chance of him tripping, unless he tied it before class was over.

Roxie's blushing had likely been his imagination, anyway. Maybe she was just queasy. That made sense. Wilmer wasn't the type to make girls blush. But queasiness? Possibly.

After all, Wilmer wasn't dashing like Zane Bradley, who sat two rows up and four seats over, just a desk away from Roxie and her friends. If only Wilmer were tall and handsome and the star dodgeball player like Zane. Wilmer's ears stuck out a bit too much, his hair was just a little too mop-like, and his front teeth were just slightly too far apart. Not that he was a total reject—Wilmer knew it was scientifically probable that he had many strengths that girls found irresistible. He just couldn't think what they might be.

Wilmer spent the rest of the period staring at his untied shoelaces.

II.

Wilmer's luck changed at lunchtime. Roxie and her friends sat at the same lunch table as Wilmer and his best friend, Ernie Rinehart. Wilmer and Ernie had sat with the girls yesterday, too. Two days in a row! Wilmer's stomach did backflips and spins as he wondered what he should say. Or maybe it was best to keep quiet. Girls liked the strong and silent type.

Wilmer felt he could manage the silent part.

Ernie noisily gulped milk from a carton. Unlike Wilmer, he was neither smallish nor hair-moppish, although his black hair did have the nasty habit of standing up to attention, as if it were saluting a flag. "Are you going to eat it or play with it?" asked Ernie, pointing to Wilmer's creamed spinach.

Wilmer picked up spinach with his fork and then dumped it back onto his plate. "I guess I'm not that hungry," he said. "Want some?"

Ernie shook his head. "No way." He lowered his milk and bit into his SugarBUZZZZ! chocolate cupcake dessert, its green frosting glowing like colored lightbulbs. Bits of glistening crumbs lingered on Ernie's fingers. "Now *that's* delicious!"

SugarBUZZZZ!—the wondrous kids' snack line that came in twelve fluorescently colored flavors—had been Wilmer's father's greatest invention. Or at least his most successful.

But while Wilmer shared his father's love for science, he didn't share his schoolmates' infatuation with sugary treats. Besides, spinach was a superfood, packed with folate and manganese— nutrients that improved brain function. A scientist always needs to be clearheaded. Science might be demanded at a moment's notice.

"You're probably the only kid in the world who eats spinach for lunch," said Ernie, licking his glowing fingers. Finished with his cupcake, he picked up his peanut butter sandwich. Ernie always ate dessert before he ate his sandwich.

"I like spinach. It's a nutritious treat," said Wilmer. "Besides, a careful analysis of your peanut butter sandwich will likely find *Rattus rattus* follicles, as well as fragments of *Periplaneta americana*."

"Speak English, please," said Ernie.

"Sorry. Rat hairs and cockroach parts. Peanut butter is loaded with them."

"I like rat hairs. That's the best part," said Ernie. He bit into his sandwich. "Yum!"

"That's just gross," said Roxie. Her voice

reminded Wilmer of a songbird floating along on a meadow breeze, or at least of how he imagined a songbird might sound if it floated on a breeze blowing in a meadow. "I just ate a peanut butter sandwich."

Wilmer took a deep breath, determined to impress Roxie with his expert food knowledge. "The federal government allows up to one rat hair per one hundred grams of peanut butter. So, statistically speaking, you may have had only one or two rat hairs in your sandwich. And peanut butter isn't as bad as pizza sauce. The government allows fly eggs in pizza sauce. And insects in chocolate. And trust me, you don't want to know what's in hot dogs."

"I had hot dogs last night for dinner," said Vonda, frowning.

"I had pizza. And some chocolate," said Roxie, holding her stomach.

"Oh. Well. Um. Fly eggs have a lot of vitamins, I think," said Wilmer, squirming. He imagined his face growing as pink as Roxie's was turning.

"You guys are disgusting," said Vonda.

Ernie peeled open his sandwich and peered

inside. "I think I see six rat hairs, four cockroach legs, and half a beetle." He closed it and held it out to Claire. "Want a bite?"

"Get that away from me!" she screamed. Claire was quite good at screaming. Ernie just laughed. Wilmer knew Ernie secretly liked Claire almost as much as Wilmer secretly liked Roxie.

"I'm eating bologna," said Vonda, taking a confident chomp of her sandwich. "Nothing wrong with this."

"Actually, most bologna has pig hearts in it. And it's wrapped in casing made from colons and intestines," said Wilmer.

Vonda put down her sandwich. "I'm never eating food again."

Ernie stared at her sandwich greedily. "Can I have it, then? I love pig hearts. Mom makes them for dinner every Thursday."

Wilmer knew he was kidding. But his comment received the desired groans and shouts of "You're sick" from Claire.

Meanwhile, Roxie's face blushed the same vibrant pink Wilmer had noticed earlier. It reminded him of a glow stick. But then it quickly faded away. Maybe the cafeteria lights were playing games with Wilmer's eyes. Wilmer needed to eat more spinach: In addition to nutrients that helped the brain, spinach also contained lutein and zeaxanthin, which improved eyesight.

When your father was a food inventor, like Wilmer's, you knew a lot about food.

"I think I'm going to throw up," said Roxie, still holding her stomach. Her face started to flash pink, on and off, not unlike a faulty neon sign.

"Pig hearts aren't so bad," said Wilmer quickly. "Some parts of the world consider them a delicacy, roasted with potatoes and garlic. My mom once made—"

"No. I mean I really have to throw up . . . ," muttered Roxie, covering her mouth and running out of the room. Vonda and Claire jumped up and quickly followed her.

"I guess they don't appreciate science," said Ernie with a smirk, biting into Vonda's sandwich.

"I guess I just don't know when to keep my mouth shut," said Wilmer with a groan.

III.

Wilmer didn't dare speak to Roxie again that day. She was back in class the next period, looking a little pinkish but otherwise normal. The day wasn't a total loss, though. After school Wilmer went to the library for some impromptu research. He decided to get a head start learning about the spread of disease in the Middle Ages. It turned out to be fascinating stuff. Long ago antibiotics and most modern-day medicines didn't exist, so new epidemics spread often and quickly. The Black Death was the worst but hardly the only disease to wipe out millions of people. In the eighteenth century smallpox killed almost sixty million Europeans, and in the early 1900s the Spanish flu killed as many as one hundred million people.

But Wilmer was starting to think that the most horrible and grossest epidemics must have happened during medieval times. Back then they seemed to pop up all over the place. Germs rapidly spread from person to person, leaving a trail of blisters, chills, fevers, blindness, gangrene, comas, skin lesions, coughs, cramps, nose decay, sweating, swelling, convulsions, headaches, vomiting, rashes, finger and toe shrinking, and other horrible things, many of which sounded even worse than death.

Wilmer imagined his ears swelling, his nose deforming, and his entire body becoming one oozing mass of bubbling rashes. Maybe Roxie would notice him then (although, he admitted, not in a good way).

To make things worse, doctors back then didn't know how to stop the diseases, or what caused them. For example, the bubonic plague spread from rats, but no one knew that until hundreds of years later.

Wilmer didn't think people were in danger of catching the Black Death from rat hairs in peanut butter, though. He hoped not. But you could never be sure what sort of epidemic was ready to spring up anywhere. One could even strike their school without warning. That was why, as a scientist, Wilmer had to be clearheaded. Just in case.

IV.

At home that evening, as he entered the kitchen, Wilmer glanced up at the small wooden sign hanging from the ceiling. It said simply, OBSERVE! Mr. Dooley had hung it years ago. It was a constant reminder of the important link between science and observation.

Wilmer swung his backpack onto the kitchen table, narrowly avoiding his seven-year-old brother, Sherman, who ran around it. Sherman, as always, was completely wired. He pretended to be a cowboy and yelled "Giddyup!" and "Yippy ki ay!" as he raced in circles. Wilmer dived out of the way to avoid being run over. Everyone else ignored him—the Dooleys were used to Sherman's mindless energy. But Wilmer couldn't help thinking that Sherman's energy today seemed even more mindless than usual.

Mrs. Dooley stood by the stove, throwing random foods into a giant pot. Short and thin, with rosy cheeks, Mrs. Dooley was always at her best around the kitchen. Or at least at her happiest. Considering all the cooking she did, it was a little surprising that she was so thin. But then, Wilmer's youngest brother, eighteen-month-old Preston, was the guinea pig taster of most of Mrs. Dooley's concoctions. And Sherman ate enough for everyone.

Standing on her tiptoes, Mrs. Dooley tossed
six whole lemons, four strips of bacon, an old comb,
half a bottle of malt vinegar, four pickles, a wrench,
and three pieces of a jigsaw puzzle into the tall pot
as she hummed the warning theme from *Jaws*, the
movie about a killer shark. *Da-dum. Da-dum.* It was
the music that played before the shark ate someone.
It was a discouraging omen. Wilmer wondered if it
meant they were all doomed if they ate dinner. The
kitchen smelled faintly like sarsaparilla, lingering
from the bizarre sarsaparilla scallop strips his
mom had whipped up a couple nights before, and
the sarsaparilla turnip muffins she had made for
lunch.

Mrs. Dooley had a particular fondness for
sarsaparilla. It had the scent of root beer, with a
hint of licorice. It smelled a lot better than some of
her other ingredients. Wilmer thought back in horror to the dreaded pickled cabbage and saffron tofu
burgers from two weeks before.

His mom continued humming away. What
she lacked in normal recipes, she made up for in
enthusiasm.

Mr. Dooley stood in the room too, washing his hands in a sink piled with dirty dishes. Scattered among Mom's bowls and graters and mixers were tubes and cups and flasks from Mr. Dooley's downstairs lab. The pile grew higher and higher throughout the day, to be washed every night only after Wilmer went to bed. He was always surprised when he came down to an empty sink at breakfast.

Tonight Mr. Dooley was wearing his lab coat inside out, and only one sock. Wilmer assumed he had spent the day hunkered down in his basement lab working on his latest invention, whatever that was. Wilmer's father kept most of what he did a complete secret. Although Mr. Dooley hadn't had any breakthroughs since SugarBUZZZZ!, he said his next invention would "revolutionize the very fabric of eating forever!"

He had said the same thing after the last six inventions, including the flying pizza, the remote control ham, and the incredible walking pudding cup, the last of which still gave Wilmer nightmares.

Mr. Dooley turned around and smiled, dripping

water onto the floor. He was tall and lanky, but forever stooped from years of peering down into microscopes. "Good morning, son," he said to Wilmer.

"It's evening, Dad," said Wilmer. "And you're dripping." A small pool of water formed next to Mr. Dooley's lone sock. Sherman, who was still sprinting around the table shouting out cowboy phrases, narrowly missed stepping in the puddle as he rounded the corner. Wilmer imagined a manic and frenzied Sherman slipping on the water, soaring into the air, and crashing into the refrigerator.

"Nice observation!" said Mr. Dooley approvingly, before bending down and wiping the puddle with a napkin. His swipe ended a split second before Sherman stepped in the exact same spot, yelling, "Rustle up the cattle, pardner!" Mrs. Dooley grabbed the napkin from Mr. Dooley's hand, sniffed it, and then threw it into the pot on the stove.

Wilmer hopped up onto the counter to avoid being barreled into as his brother rounded the corner again.

Meanwhile, Preston Dooley sat in his high chair at the kitchen table. Mrs. Dooley removed what appeared to be a shoe from her pot and handed it to her youngest son, who gnawed on it.

"Orange zest!" screamed Preston.

"Wonderful idea," sang Mrs. Dooley, tossing three oranges into the pot. Wilmer wished he had eaten all his creamed spinach at lunch, rather than playing with it. He was not looking forward to dinner.

"I call it Soupy Shoe Surprise," said Mrs. Dooley as she ladled dinner into bowls. "With a hint of orange zest."

"Orange zest!" squealed Preston with pride.

"What's the surprise in Soupy Shoe Surprise?" asked Wilmer.

"If we can eat it without getting sick!" exclaimed Mrs. Dooley. Wilmer wasn't sure if she was joking.

The family sat down around the table. Sherman bounced on his chair; even when sitting, the boy couldn't stop moving. Preston slurped his soup with great enthusiasm.

Wilmer looked into his bowl. His purplish green glop made disturbing slurping noises.

"You've done it again, Maggie," said Mr. Dooley with a warm grin and a lick of his lips. "Delicious! So, Wilmer. You're going to win the science medal this year, right? Any ideas yet?"

The sixth-grade end-of-year ceremony neared, along with the coveted Mumpley Sixth-Grade Science Medal. Awarded to the top student science entry, it was the most prestigious of all the sixth-grade awards. Mr. Dooley had won it when he was in school, and he expected Wilmer to follow in his footsteps. The trophy was displayed proudly among Mr. Dooley's many science awards on the mantel over the fireplace.

"I have an assignment at school with possibilities," said Wilmer. "We're studying Middle Ages diseases."

"Like when your hair starts growing in weird places and your knees hurt for no reason?" asked Mr. Dooley.

"No, I mean diseases from the Middle Ages. Not diseases you get when you're middle aged."

"Oh. Too bad," said Mr. Dooley, who plucked a hair from his nose and sniffled.

Wilmer shook his head and looked into his soup. It still bubbled and burped, but Wilmer's stomach growled even louder, so he risked a taste.

He had to admit, it was pretty good. The orange zest added just the right kick.

V.

After dinner Mr. Dooley stretched out on his recliner and waved Wilmer over, inviting him to sit on the ottoman. Mr. Dooley's thick, black-rimmed glasses made his eyes seem twice as big as they were. Whenever he saw his father, Wilmer vowed to eat even more eye-boosting spinach than ever.

"What do I always say, son?"

"'Where are my car keys?'"

"Yes, well, besides that. Observe! That's what makes great scientists. We can learn plenty from observation, son." Mr. Dooley leaned back on the leather seat. "Have I told you that the idea for my fluorescent snack line, SugarBUZZZZ!, came from observing fireflies?"

"Only two hundred sixteen times."

"Yes, there I was," said Mr. Dooley, staring out

the window and lost in thought. "Outside, sneezing. I was allergic to flowers and wondered what would happen if I crammed an entire flower up my nose. It was a poorly conceived experiment. But then a firefly flew by. Of course I knew they glow because luciferins combine with oxygen to form oxyluciferin, and so on. But I was drinking orange soda at the time, which proved to be extremely difficult while sneezing and holding a flower in my nose, and I wondered what would happen if my drink glowed. And the rest is history."

"That's really interesting, Dad," said Wilmer, yawning and looking at his cuticles.

"The point is, um . . . I forget. That glowing orange soda is much more fun than regular soda?"

"I thought the point was observation."

"Right, that's what I meant. Thank you." Mr. Dooley's absentmindedness was legendary in the Dooley household. "Observation! That's what makes great science. I bet you could use this Middle Ages unit as a jumping-off point for some new perspectives on our world today. Look around you. Observe! You'll have a great new idea for a science experiment in no time. The Mumpley Sixth-Grade Science Medal awaits!"

Wilmer nodded. He needed to start his own trophy collection. He hated staring at Dad's award shelf all day long. After all, Wilmer wasn't getting any younger. Mozart composed music when he was only five years old! Picasso completed his first painting when he was only eight! At eleven years old, Wilmer was an old man compared with them. It was about time he carved a path for himself.

Of course, Wilmer also thought about Roxie. Girls admired guys who won trophies, even more than guys who gave flowers. Maybe winning the medal would impress her. He couldn't be strong, but he had his brain, and that counted for something. At least, he hoped it did.

He just needed a great science project idea for his entry.

Wilmer looked at Sherman, who once again raced around the kitchen table. He squinted. Had Sherman's ears begun to glow yellow? He wasn't completely sure. Wilmer sat back and observed.

THURSDAY
Day 3

Dear Journal,

    My plans to win Roxie's affections with poetry came to an abrupt end when I couldn't find a rhyme for "lower intestine." The poem, titled "I Love You with All My Heart and Various Internal Organs," was off to a promising start too. "You will always be my queen, and I love you from my spleen." Also, "My love for you is far-flung. For you, I'd cough up a lung." You don't find lines like those just anywhere.

    Maybe that's a good thing.

    I suppose my plan to mix sonnets with science might have been flawed. But that meant I had extra time to observe!

    I observed some interesting developments this morning.

    Roxie is pink, as pink as she appeared yesterday, and it's not from blushing. She's just pink. It looks good on her, though. It matches her green eyes exceptionally well.

Other than her pink shade and some rather mild cold symptoms, however, she seems completely normal. For example, she still barely notices me at all.

Ernie is coming down with something too. He sneezed three times before class this morning, and his nose briefly turned bright green each time. I believe there may have been traces of green glow on his tissue. I'll grab a sample for testing as soon as possible.

Vonda Binkowski also sniffled. Ernie asked if she had found any rat hairs in her dinner last night, and she stuck her tongue out at him. Interestingly, it was orange.

I'll observe the rest of the class closely today to see if they also exhibit strange symptoms. With a bit of luck I'll draw some solid scientific conclusions.

But then, there's no such thing as luck; luck is purely the statistical increase of positive results by bumped into her and not the other way around. Wilmer bent down and picked her cherry pits out of the waste container. Each one glowed with a slight orange tint, just as he suspected they might. These went into a second plastic bag. They were worth a closer inspection at home too.

This was the strangest cold that Wilmer had ever seen. Comparing diseases from the Middle Ages with this curious strain of twenty-first-century bacteria might be the perfect basis for his history project, and for his science medal entry.

He patted his backpack, gave a small but enthusiastic pump of his fist, and headed to class.

II.

What was that boy up to? Valveeta Padgett, biology teacher for fifteen years, chair of the school Science Department, co-chair of the school Detention Program, and co-co-chair of the school Chair Cleaning Committee, lingered by the front cafeteria doors. Wilmer strolled past her as he exited the cafeteria. Valveeta Padgett didn't trust that kid, not one bit. He never did his assigned reading, yet somehow he putting yourself into a likely situation. Although that doesn't explain why I'm not having any luck with Roxie.

Signing off,
Wilmer Dooley

I.

Wilmer removed the lock protecting the surprisingly spacious science compartment in his backpack. He unzipped the pocket, took out the rubber gloves from inside it, and unrolled them. A scientist always takes great pains to avoid contaminating evidence, or himself. Gloves on, Wilmer lifted one of Ernie's used tissues from the lunchroom trashcan. A greenish glowing smear stained it. Wilmer carefully sealed the tissue inside a small plastic bag. He could test Ernie's DNA in his lab at home.

Vonda Binkowski sniffled and accidentally banged into Wilmer's arm as she spit two cherry pits into the garbage. She lingered only long enough to grunt and give Wilmer a dirty look, as if he had bumped into her and not the other way around. Wilmer bent down and picked her cherry pits out of the waste container. Each one glowed with a slight orange tint, just as he suspected they might. These went into a second plastic bag. They were worth a closer inspection at home too.

This was the strangest cold that Wilmer had ever seen. Comparing diseases from the Middle Ages with this curious strain of twenty-first-century bacteria might be the perfect basis for his history project, and for his science medal entry.

He patted his backpack, gave a small but enthusiastic pump of his fist, and headed to class.

II.

What was that boy up to? Valveeta Padgett, biology teacher for fifteen years, chair of the school Science Department, co-chair of the school Detention Program, and co-co-chair of the school Chair Cleaning Committee, lingered by the front cafeteria doors. Wilmer strolled past her as he exited the cafeteria. Valveeta Padgett didn't trust that kid, not one bit. He never did his assigned reading, yet somehow he knew even more about biology than she did. Valveeta Padgett didn't like kids who knew more than her about anything, and especially about biology. She had a degree from a very good university, thank you, and had written and published three papers on the biological diversity of snails. Quite impressive. But what had this pip-squeak Wilmer Dooley accomplished, other than being lucky enough to have a father who became wealthy by selling sugary snacks to kids? Nothing, that's what.

Wilmer was messy, too, and Valveeta Padgett, co-co-chair of the school Chair Cleaning Committee, was very particular about messiness and orderliness. That was quite obvious from her immaculately crisp black skirts and perfectly coiffed hair bun. Wilmer always left the smell of sulfur behind after his classroom lab assignments, even from those assignments that didn't require sulfur. Also, his experiments often exploded for no apparent reason. She still didn't understand how he blew up Franklin Jones's backpack while dissecting a frog.

But worst of all, Mrs. Padgett had spied Wilmer using her science equipment after school without permission on a half dozen occasions, and fourteen test tubes were still missing from the supply cabinet. She had been missing fifteen, but she found one under her desk last week. She couldn't prove Wilmer Dooley had stolen those fourteen vanished test tubes, but he was the most obvious culprit.

She just needed proof that he was a thief.

A few weeks ago Mrs. Padgett had set up a camera in the lab to catch his thievery. But Wilmer was too clever. She suspected he was well aware of the camera, since in the middle of his experiment he turned, bowed, and danced a jig.

So Mrs. Padgett scrapped the camera idea. She would catch him with her own two eyes! She began hiding in the closet during lunchtime. Mrs. Padgett was quite tall, even taller with her high hair bun, so hiding in a closet was not a simple thing to do. After two weeks it seemed that her patience and sore back would finally be rewarded when Wilmer sneaked into the classroom again. But the boy took nothing. What was he doing? The boy bowed and did another jig. Maybe the boy just liked to jig. She trusted jigging boys even less than those who did science experiments unannounced and unapproved.

Confused but irate, she had approached Principal Shropshire about Wilmer's uninvited lab lurking. She neglected to mention the jigging. As chair of the school Science Department, co-chair of the school Detention Program, and co-co-chair of the school Chair Cleaning Committee, she had a responsibility to bring suspicious activities to his attention.

But he had barely cared! Principal Shropshire chuckled in that annoying, bumbling way of his. Worse, he seemed impressed by Wilmer's academic enthusiasm and suggested that the boy be left to his own devices.

While they talked, Principal Shropshire had drunk a large glass of glowing yellow Lemon-BUZZZZ! so Mrs. Padgett suspected his loyalties might be misguided. Didn't he understand that test tubes were missing? That 6.3 percent of Mrs. Padgett's precious supply of cowitch powder had disappeared?

So that conversation had been quite unfruitful.

But someday she would catch Wilmer doing something horrible, and that would be the end of his sneakiness.

Now, at the cafeteria doors, Mrs. Padgett was watching Wilmer walk down the hall when someone else caught her eye. Claudius Dill. Why was he lurking in the shadows and spying on Wilmer with shifty eyes and a scowl on his face? Claudius Dill! Now, *that* boy had a future! Sure, the box of chocolates he bought her for her birthday was unnecessary, as was his insistence on staying late on Fridays to clean her whiteboard. But he was industrious! Helpful! A bit of a suck-up, but what's wrong with sucking up every now and then? Mrs. Valveeta Padgett deserved a little sucking up to. Maybe if Wilmer Dooley sucked up more often, he would not be such a disgrace.

Besides, Claudius Dill wasn't all jumpy and scatterbrained like some of the other kids in her classes. He had a severe SugarBUZZZZ! allergy, so the boy never touched any glowing foods. It made her trust him even more.

Claudius emerged from his hiding place and glanced around. He saw Mrs. Padgett watching him, and his scowl vanished, replaced with a smile that looked somewhat fake. Then he hurried off.

He was up to something. Mrs. Padgett knew Claudius Dill and Wilmer Dooley were rivals. They were both anxious to get the Sixth-Grade Science Medal.

Mrs. Padgett quietly rooted for Claudius to be victorious. Since she was chair of the school Science Department, the winner was her final decision. And there was no way she was handing that trophy to Wilmer Dooley.

"Good day, Mrs. Padgett," said Mr. Churtles, the head of the school lunchroom. He held a number of small empty milk cartons to toss away. "The cafeteria is closing. Would you like to grab some lunch first?"

"No," said Mrs. Padgett, turning on her tall black heels. "I think I'll skip lunch today. I have some thinking to do."

III.

Most of Wilmer's history class met in the library that afternoon during study hall so that they could research their medieval history papers. Ernie and

Wilmer managed to wiggle their way into seats at Roxie, Vonda, and Claire's table.

Excited, they wrapped their thumbs together. That was their secret best-friend handshake, or rather thumbshake, and had been since the third grade, when they made their vows to be lifelong friends, no matter what.

Wilmer found it hard to concentrate. Instead of working, he kept sneaking peeks at Roxie. His heart sped. His normal heartbeat was approximately 91 beats per minute, but Wilmer timed his current heartrate racing at an alarming 132 beats, an increase of 45 percent.

He immediately stared down at his notes whenever he sensed Roxie might look up. Wilmer was getting seasick from constantly looking up and down, up and down.

Ernie cleared his throat and held up his book. "Back in medieval times some doctors thought diseases came from evil spirits living in your head. They cut a hole in your skull to release them."

"I think you have a hole in your skull," said Claire.

Unfazed, Ernie continued, looking deeply into Claire's eyes as he talked. "I'm not kidding. It also says doctors loved leeching patients. Leeches are disgusting, slimy worms that suck blood."

"Sort of like you," said Vonda.

"Only you're way more slimy," chimed in Claire.

"I vant to suck your blood!" said Ernie in a bad Dracula accent. The girls all rolled their eyes, but Wilmer laughed.

"That's because they didn't have reporters like Gwendolyn Bray back then. She would have exposed the truth about those quack doctors," said Roxie.

Gwendolyn Bray was the star reporter of the local TV station, channel 8 (channel 268 in HD). It was no secret that Roxie idolized her. Every other Monday, Roxie McGhee hosted the *Monday Mumpley Musings* radio show, which was broadcast throughout the school. She always ended with the same sign-off that Gwendolyn Bray used:

"And that's nothing but the truth!"

Ernie sneezed loudly, startling everyone at the

table. His nose glowed green for a brief moment. His tissue glowed too, like radioactive waste. He held it up and waved it near Claire's face. "Pretty cool, huh?"

Claire batted his hand away. "No. It's pretty gross. Get that away!"

"Watch this!" said Ernie. He blew his nose as hard as he could. It turned a particularly bright neon chartreuse. It remained glowing for a good ten seconds.

"Look! It's Ernie the green-nosed doofus!" said Claire. Vonda and Roxie laughed.

Ernie stood up, his face blushing. But blushing green. "I need to find more books for my project," he mumbled as the girls continued to giggle. He pushed his chair away from the table and stomped off, his hand covering his nose.

As he walked away, Ernie sneezed. His nose flashed brightly through his fingers. Wilmer watched with curiosity. He had never heard of a cold that turned your nose green.

The girls continued laughing.

"Leeches were pretty common back then," said

Wilmer, trying to change the subject so that the trio would stop giggling at his friend. "I've read that doctors used to put as many as fifty leeches on someone at once. They thought the worms would suck out the disease." He put an eraser on his arm. "Imagine this is a leech sucking out my blood—"

"No thanks," said Vonda, turning away.

"You're grosser than Ernie," said Claire.

"I think I'm feeling nauseous again," said Roxie, puffing her cheeks out. Her pink face started to glow again. "Excuse me!"

"I wasn't trying to be gross. I was just explaining how leeches suck through your skin . . . ," began Wilmer, but it was too late. Roxie rushed out of the room. Claire and Vonda followed behind her. Wilmer shook his head. Once again he had said a bit too much.

Girls liked the silent type. He needed to stop forgetting that.

IV.

When Wilmer arrived home after school, he dashed up the stairs and straight to his room. He flipped the sign on his door from WELCOME to DO NOT DISTURB, SCIENCE IN PROGRESS. He closed the door and locked it.

Wilmer had transformed his desk into a mini lab with a magnifying glass, a scale, weights and measures, and a few other basic science tools, such as the fourteen test tubes he swore he would return to school someday. They were just borrowed. All scientists need test tubes.

His desktop lab was only for quick fieldwork, though; he didn't have the space or resources for more intensive studies. His magnifying glass wasn't very powerful, and the Bunsen burner didn't get very hot. Wilmer wished he could use his dad's state-of-the-art basement laboratory, but Mr. Dooley had a very strict NO ONE ALLOWED EXCEPT ME sign on the door. So Wilmer did most of his serious experiments in Mrs. Padgett's classroom at school. Just the other month he was working on an anti-itching cream, inspired by a rather severe bout of poison ivy. Unfortunately, the cream made Wilmer itch even more. Worse, Wilmer accidentally spilled some of the cowitch powder he was using into his pants. He began dancing around in a weird jig, scratching desperately. Then the exact same thing happened two weeks later! He was just glad no one saw him. He thought he heard someone hiding in Mrs. Padgett's closet during his second jig, but realized that was ridiculous.

He slipped on his lab coat. It had been Mr. Dooley's long ago. Wilmer needed to roll up the sleeves because they were too long, but wearing the coat made him feel scientific. He loved feeling scientific.

Wilmer put the samples on his desk: two cherry pits; one tissue. They both still glimmered from their bright colors. This was the strangest cold Wilmer had ever seen. He quickly ripped a piece of paper from his scientific notebook binder and wrote in big letters: "The Present-Day Plague." He taped it over his desk.

Maybe he was being silly. It took more than two or three people for something to be called a plague; maybe it was just your standard, everyday cold with some strange, color-glowing side effects. Besides, Ernie and Roxie didn't have symptoms

you would normally associate with a plague. Ernie wasn't acting strangely, at least not any stranger than usual (when he wasn't around Claire Huddleston). Roxie was still her beautiful, glorious self too, except for her queasiness.

But the more he thought about it, the more Wilmer was convinced that comparing this new strain of cold with diseases of the Middle Ages might be a great entry for that Sixth-Grade Science Medal. The perfect start for his own trophy collection over the fireplace.

He just needed to observe!

And think a bit.

Wilmer went downstairs. Sherman ran around the kitchen table screaming cowboy chants, like "There's a new sheriff in town!" and "Hi-ho, Silver!" Mr. Dooley was still locked away in his basement working on who knew what. Preston sat on the floor tasting a variety of odd foods, some of which wiggled, others that looked like tree bark, and others that seemed like stripes of toothpaste. Occasionally he would scream out random foods, like "Vanilla!" or "Guacamole!" and Mrs. Dooley would nod eagerly and add some new ingredients to one of the pots bubbling on the stove.

A large flame erupted from the tallest pot, but Mrs. Dooley quickly dulled it by standing on a stepladder and spraying it with the small fire extinguisher she always kept nearby. She shrugged, dipped her finger into the broth, and then stirred, fire extinguisher foam and all. She whistled merrily the entire time.

Wilmer sighed. Just another evening in the Dooley kitchen. To avoid the commotion, Wilmer decided to keep his distance. He went into the family room to sit on his dad's recliner. He stared at his father's mantel of trophies, lost in thought and possibility.

FRIDAY
Day 4

Dear Journal,

I've found many scientific journals devoted to medieval diseases and especially the bubonic plague. It's quite fascinating. The plague spread quickly and wiped out tens of millions of people before vanishing. Symptoms included high fever, chills, and bleeding from the ears. The disease popped back up every few years, killing millions more people every time. No one could stop it. No one even figured out what caused it until more than four hundred years later.

Love is like an epidemic, sort of. It invades your body like bacteria and won't go away, whether you want it to or not. Every time Roxie smiles, my stomach cramps, my hands start to shake, and I'm covered in sweat. Interestingly, those are the same symptoms I had after trying Mom's horrifying jalapeño bread pudding last month.

I'm not sure if I can officially call this bizarre, colorful cold that is spreading through our school an epidemic yet, but it sure feels like one. Especially after what I observed this morning before first period.

Most of the sixth-grade class was hanging out in the school yard, like usual. Ernie and I were spying on Roxie, Claire, and Vonda, also like usual. Ernie's nose was now a continual bright green, as was the rest of his head. Unfortunately, this made it harder to spy—it was like hiding under a bright neon sign. Roxie was bright pink from her head to her flip-flop-wearing feet, and Vonda's orange had spread from her tongue to her face. I quickly jotted notes into my journal. It was quite curious, to say the least.

Behind us a chorus of girls screamed, "Ewww!" and, "Get away!" Boys shouted, "Cool!" and, "Check it out!" and, "Do that again!" Obviously, this piqued my scientific interest.

It turned out that Ronny Roswick had just vomited in the middle of the school yard. But that wasn't the strange part. Ronny throws up every now and again. He has a weak stomach.

The strange part was this: The vomit was bright, glowing purple, as was half of Ronny's head!

There was pandemonium in the school yard. Ronny took off like a bottle rocket and ran laps around the yard. Meanwhile, a group of girls pointed to the purple puke and shrieked, while the boys exchanged high fives. Two boys chased after Ronny, and when they returned, they both were dripping violet-colored beads of sweat.

Mr. Havendash finally corralled Ronny and led him into the building to see the nurse. Ronny fidgeted the entire time, as if his legs were anxious to continue running in circles.

This is certainly not your run-of-the mill, everyday bug! It's a mystery that needs to be solved, a scientific pretzel that demands the brightest mind to untwist.

And I can't think of a scientific mind more up to the challenge than mine.

The fate of the school might depend on me:

Ernie's nose, Ronny's puke, Vonda's tongue, and most importantly, Roxie's pink head.

I only hope I'm not in over my own head.

Signing off,
Wilmer Dooley

I.

The sixth graders filed into the school's sixth-grade wing from the yard. Class was starting any minute, but Wilmer stayed behind. He unlocked his secret scientific backpack compartment, unzipped the pocket, and removed the face mask he had placed in it the night before. He couldn't take any chances around this colorful contagion. After all, he didn't know how the disease spread and what long-term damage it caused.

It seemed rather harmless so far. But who knew what could happen next?

Wilmer dipped a wooden tongue depressor into the vomit and swirled it around. He lifted a large, chunky, and dripping piece. Wilmer's face mask kept most of the odor from his nose, but purple vomit still smelled like vomit, and vomit still smelled strongly horrible. Wilmer was glad when the sample was safely sealed inside a plastic bag. As he walked back to the school building, strands of barf stink lingered in his nostrils.

Wilmer wasn't the only one still in the school yard. Claudius Dill hung from the monkey bars, watching. Wilmer glanced at him, narrowing his eyes. He trusted Claudius as far as he could spit, which was exactly a wind-aided thirty-four inches, according to Wilmer's spit distance research last year.

Wilmer glared at Claudius. Claudius glared back. Wilmer had good reason to be suspicious of Claudius Dill. Last semester Copernicus, the history-class iguana, had been very sick, but no one knew why. Wilmer vowed to solve the mystery. During recess he examined the grungy contents of Copernicus's food, while Claudius lurked in the back of the room. But the answer jumped out at Wilmer. Literally. A cricket leaped up and smacked him in the eye. What was a cricket doing in Copernicus's food? Wilmer knew eating crickets was harmful to a vegetarian iguana's health.

When Wilmer went to the bathroom to wash off his eyeball (which stung from the cricket ramming into it), Claudius took all the credit. He told everyone that *he* had discovered what was making the old lizard ill. No one believed that Wilmer had cracked the case. Wilmer suspected that Claudius had been feeding Copernicus the crickets all along, but he couldn't prove it. Now Wilmer always kept his eyes open for Claudius, while also being careful a cricket wouldn't jump into them at the same time.

Claudius was Wilmer's greatest threat to winning the Sixth-Grade Science Medal. Not because Claudius was a better scientist. Wilmer could out-science Claudius any day of the week. No, Claudius was a threat because he cheated.

But Wilmer knew that science had no place for cheaters. Science was about fact, not fiction.

II.

Claudius watched Wilmer, his eyes slits of burning hatred. What was that sniveling science wannabe doing with that vomit? Wilmer pranced around like he knew everything—doing experiments, finding carefully concealed crickets in iguana food, and generally acting like he was more intelligent than everyone else.

But being smarter didn't matter. Being smarter didn't win Sixth-Grade Science Medals. What was most important was being sneakier. And no one was sneakier than Claudius Dill.

Claudius watched as Wilmer locked his backpack. What did he plan to do with that vomit sample? Claudius had been intrigued too. You don't see bright purple puke every day.

What was Wilmer's game? That was another reason Claudius despised him. Wilmer didn't do his science experiments for any reason other than for the sake of science.

Despicable!

What was the sense of inventing something if you couldn't turn a profit? Why stay after school if you didn't want to sell your discoveries to the highest bidder? What was the point of spending every Friday cleaning a biology teacher's whiteboards if you didn't plan on using it later to your advantage?

Wilmer's dad had made a small fortune from SugarBUZZZZ! That was also a problem. He'd made a *small* fortune! If Claudius had invented that sugary stuff, he would have made a *gigantic* fortune!

Wilmer didn't have a monopoly on successful dads. Claudius's father was the World's Greatest Doctor, according to *Medicine Today* magazine, and continuously traveled around the world giving lectures. One year he visited eighty-eight countries! Claudius saw his father only four days that year, and on three of those days he saw him only at breakfast. But you make sacrifices for success, such as spending every weekend for two months looking for small-size crickets to hide in iguana food. Claudius was willing to sacrifice anyone—or anything—to get what he wanted.

Evil geniuses had the right idea. They created sinister gadgets and plotted mischievous schemes to get rich. Claudius fancied himself an evil genius in waiting. He even owned a T-shirt that said EVIL GENIUS, although he wore it only when he was alone in his bedroom, or sometimes beneath a sweater.

As he stared at Wilmer, Claudius mustered the most maniacal, hateful look he could imagine, trying to send out evil thoughts that would creep into Wilmer's brain and make it explode! Nothing happened, but it wasn't from a lack of trying. He'd show Wilmer. Claudius was going to win the Sixth-Grade Science Medal and put Wilmer in his two-bit science place. And maybe, if he played his cards right, he could do it while turning a profit.

Once Wilmer was back inside the school, Claudius swung down from the monkey bars. As he did, he saw Mrs. Padgett looking down from the second-floor window, scowling at the mound of reeking vomit. She was a valuable ally. Claudius made a mental note to clean her whiteboard twice this week, instead of the usual once.

III.

Mrs. Dooley prepared dinner as recklessly and haphazardly as usual. Since she never wrote down her recipes, the Dooleys never ate the same meal twice. That was generally fine with Wilmer, since most of Mom's meals were rather unpleasant. Still, she occasionally hit upon some combination of flavors that sang in harmony. Too bad she never remembered what they were, so those tasteful songs were lost forever. Preston shouted, "Almond vinegar! Watermelon seeds! Tea bags!" and in they went, flying into the air, buzzing over Sherman's head as he raced around the kitchen table.

Mr. Dooley stood by the kitchen sink, washing his hands, as he did every night, amid the kitchen crockery and laboratory petri dishes. He was very exacting about hand washing. Mr. Dooley said it was important for scientists to have clean hands so that they didn't contaminate experiments. You never know when the opportunity for an experiment might pop up.

"I wish you would put your lab dishes somewhere else," said Mrs. Dooley, looking over. "I'm always mixing them up with the dinner plates."

"Science is a dirty business," said Mr. Dooley. He held up his hands. "But not now. Nice and clean."

"Dinner is ready!" shouted Mrs. Dooley. "I think. As ready as it will ever be, I suppose. It's really hard to say." In response the vat of broth on the stove burped.

Sherman hopped into his seat. Wilmer sat down next to him. Mrs. Dooley ladled them each the debatably edible meal of okra–passion fruit–gizzard gumbo. Its dull gray color sat like a stagnant pool of mud. Wilmer closed his eyes. This meal would be better eaten blindfolded.

But eating with his eyes closed proved to be a challenge. Wilmer kept missing his mouth with his spoon, and instead repeatedly jabbed his cheek and chin. "You know, Mom," he said, after finally finding his mouth and swallowing, "this isn't as bad as it looks."

"What? I can't hear you with your eyes closed," said Mrs. Dooley.

Wilmer opened his eyes and repeated his compliment. Mr. Dooley smiled as Wilmer finished the bowl, squinting.

But Wilmer skipped dessert. He wasn't a dessert kind of person since dessert lacked proper nutritional value. Preston shared his brother's distaste for sweets. Sherman, however, didn't. The seven-year-old dug into his glowing cupcake, his mouth a blur of quick-chomping jaw muscles. He ate his cupcake in 4.2 seconds, according to Wilmer's watch.

Wilmer rose from his chair to head up to his bedroom lab.

"Wilmer! Come here!" Mr. Dooley motioned for Wilmer to join him in the family room. He sat on his favorite recliner, and Wilmer squeezed onto the ottoman next to his father's monkey-slipper-clad feet.

"Wilmer, my boy!" shouted Mr. Dooley. "I've been thinking about what we discussed the other day." Wilmer sat still, waiting for his father to continue. Finally, after scratching his head for a few seconds, Mr. Dooley said, "What did we discuss, again?"

"Medieval diseases? The Sixth-Grade Science Medal?" suggested Wilmer. They had also discussed the importance of flossing, but Wilmer doubted that's what his father had in mind.

"Exactly that!" said Mr. Dooley, straightening his glasses. "Have you made any progress? Have you been observing? Science is all about observation, you know."

Wilmer nodded. "I think so, Dad. There's a cold going around school that's really interesting. I'd planned to compare it with medieval diseases, but I'm not completely sure yet."

"Outstanding! Remember, science is about the endless pursuit of the truth. Hunt it tirelessly with no regard to your personal hygiene! Why, sometimes when I'm involved in a new project, I don't shower for weeks. Will you do that, Wilmer?"

"You don't want me to shower for weeks? I think Mom will get mad."

"No! Bathe as you wish. I mean, will you doggedly pursue the truth? Will you make me proud?" Wilmer nodded. Mr. Dooley patted Wilmer on the back and then gestured to the trophies on the mantel. "Did I ever tell you how I won my Sixth-Grade Science Medal?"

"Yes," said Wilmer, twiddling this thumbs.

"It was a stroke of genius," said Mr. Dooley, ignoring Wilmer's rotating digits. "I investigated the effect sugar has on slugs. As you might know, salt kills slugs through dehydration. But no one had tested what effect sugar might have on those slimy little buggers. You might not think it would have much effect at all, but those very early investigations led to more sugar experiments, and those eventually inspired SugarBUZZZZ! And, um, Grandpa helped a little. The science medal might change your life, Wilmer—just like it has mine. Observe! Investigate! Your whole future may hang in the balance!"

"Great. Uh-huh. Fascinating. Can I go now?"

Mr. Dooley nodded. Wilmer stood up to leave. Still, there was one thing that struck Wilmer about his father's story, something he had never asked despite the eighty-seven times he had heard his father tell it.

"Dad, I know how your sixth-grade experiment detailed the effect of sugar on slugs. But you've never told me: What does it actually do to them?"

"Nothing at all. But the world may never have known that fact if I hadn't done my experiment."

Wilmer sighed and bounded up the stairs to his room to observe. Observation didn't observe itself, after all.

IV.

Behind his closed bedroom door Wilmer placed the samples from school on his desk: a test tube of purple vomit, two orange-tinged cherry pits, and a green, snot-smeared tissue. Lastly, but best of all, he gingerly laid down two strands of pink hair that had fallen from Roxie's comb. Wilmer had quickly snatched them from the classroom floor with the tweezers he carried in his pocket.

On his bed Wilmer laid out a number of additional items he had gathered: grass, an eye patch, a pair of dentures that Grandma had left last time she visited, dish soap, shredded rutabaga coupons, and some okra–passion fruit–gizzard gumbo cradled in a napkin.

Wilmer sucked purple puke into a syringe. He wondered what might happen if he squirted it onto each item. He hoped for some sort of chemical reaction. That might just be the clue he needed.

Wilmer spurted three drops of vomit onto a blade of grass and waited. Nothing happened.

He dripped the vomit onto the eye patch. Again there was no reaction. He knew it was unlikely that eye patches had spread the contagion, but great science never makes assumptions. Wilmer then drizzled vomit onto the dentures, dish soap, and shredded-rutabaga coupons, but each did the same thing, which was nothing. Finally Wilmer tried the gumbo. Immediately the vomit began to bubble, frothing up into a little gurgling mass and then spurting four inches into the air.

Observation!

Something about the gumbo had interacted with the glowing vomit. That might mean the plague was food related. But how? What was in the gumbo, anyway? Homegrown okra. Tomatoes. A pinch of SugarBUZZZZ! A tennis ball. There was no telling what else had been thrown in. Mrs. Dooley wouldn't remember, either.

Still, this was a major development. Food! It could have come from the lunchroom, someone's lunch bag, a snack, or practically anywhere. But it eliminated so many possibilities, such as those involving eye patches and dentures.

Wilmer realized that comparing this disease with a medieval epidemic wasn't the most important thing to worry about right now. This was no doubt a brand-new disease, a food-borne menace that needed his undivided attention.

He needed to discover this new disease's origin. But he couldn't stop there. He also needed to find a cure. It might be the first step down the path to scientific greatness.

Wilmer would cure the contagious colors of Mumpley Middle School!

He would win the Sixth-Grade Science Medal too. And maybe, if he was lucky, he would win Roxie's vibrantly pink, pulsing heart—all of it, from the aorta to the left ventricle.

MONDAY
Day 7

Dear Journal,

Over the weekend I researched diseases that change skin color. Chicken pox creates red dots. Jaundice causes yellow skin and eyes. Cyanosis can turn the skin bluish. But I've found nothing that matches the alarming transmogrifications happening in school.

I wasn't able to research for as long as I had hoped. Mom forced me to take Sherman to the park, where he raced around the monkey bars for two hours without stopping, and then reversed direction and ran for another hour. Still, I took notes. By the time he was finished, his ears had turned an alarming royal blue. Mom and Dad don't seem to be aware of it. Mom cooked all weekend, and Dad spent his time working downstairs. When

Dad finally came up after a full day in his lab, his shirt was backward and he wasn't wearing pants.

Noticing something like Sherman's blue ears might have been asking a bit too much of them.

If Preston noticed the baffling color change, he didn't say. He was busy tasting Mom's newest experiments in Cheez Whiz.

But diseases don't take weekends off, even if science must. School looked like a bright crayon box this morning, with nearly everyone glowing in assorted colors. Mandy Wilkerson is a cool winter-green, Tommy Dorps is a bright amber, and Peter Wagner is a robust ruby.

Nearly half the grade didn't come to school, probably either because they are sick or because their parents want to keep them from becoming that way. In fact, by my calculations, 48.2 percent of the sixth-grade class is absent today. Those that are in attendance are not only as colorful as a bag of Skittles, but continually sneeze, cough, and wheeze. A few vomit, but that symptom seems to be fading. No one is complaining, though. It seems that most kids would rather be bright orange and sneezing than their boring normal skin color. But I'm glad I'm unaffected. It's easier to observe when you're not magenta.

Unfortunately, I must put my attempts to win Roxie on hold while I investigate this strange contagion. It's just as well. She sneezed and I offered her a tissue, hoping she might appreciate my thoughtfulness. But I accidentally grabbed a tissue with an orange snot smear (that I had collected for later study). Roxie frowned, called me gross, and ran away, while I vainly reached for a booger-free nose-wiping option.

My romantic hopes grow dimmer. If only they shone as brightly as the sky blue Elvira Menkin racing through the halls.

But just as strange as the bursting colors is the wild, out-of-control restlessness. My classmates sprint in circles or jog in place, practically exploding with extra energy. Ernie did sit-ups this morning as we spied on Roxie and her friends. When I asked him to knock it off, he did jumping jacks instead.

I can't help but think that all this energy is

related to the mysterious pathogen, although I'm not sure how. I need to connect the dots. I need to cram in plenty of observation. The school is counting on me. Roxie is counting on me, even if she doesn't know it.

Signing off,
Wilmer Dooley

I.

Wilmer walked gingerly, carefully avoiding his sprinting, spinning, leaping classmates. It was as if they had turned into larger versions of his hyper brother Sherman. An impromptu game of leapfrog erupted in the hallway, and Wilmer was one of the few students uninterested in joining. The Chen twins were particularly impressive leapfroggers, with Charlie Chen—or was it his identical brother, Chuck?—launching himself so high he broke the overhead fluorescent light with his purple fluorescent head. Wilmer had to hug the wall to avoid being leaped on.

But still Wilmer observed. The coughing and sneezing seemed to be more of an inconvenience than a problem. Despite the cold-like symptoms, the surge in energy and the sparkling shades seemed to have everyone in good spirits. Everyone but Mr. Tuttle, at least. Twice, Wilmer saw the school nurse shaking his head and muttering to himself as he escorted multicolored kids with skinned knees and bruises down the hall to his office.

"Please, be careful," he said to the chartreuse-covered Felix Frostmire, who was chicken-fighting with an electric purple Cody Bimble and a shamrock-tinted Jason Mertz. "Kids! Get down from there!" he pleaded to a mustardy Mason All-bright, who swung dangerously from a door frame while banging his chest and grunting like a gorilla.

Wilmer scribbled his observations into his notebook as quickly as he could. Two orange girls nearly ran him over.

"Mom almost made me stay home today," said the apricot-tinged Bella Bimms.

"Me too," agreed the pumpkin-toned Gabi

Lersh. "But I wouldn't miss this for the world. I hope I can go to school tomorrow!"

"I'm going to do extra homework tonight so that Mom thinks I have a test in the morning."

"That's a good idea. I'll race you to class!"

Off the two girls went, sprinting down the hall. Wilmer barely avoided being trampled. He added these fresh observations to his journal.

At lunch Ernie bounced on his seat like an excited hamster waiting his turn on the spinning wheel. Wilmer grew exhausted watching Ernie bop up and down.

"This weekend was awesome!" said Ernie in between bounces. "I sneezed so hard that I shot a giant glowing green lugie across my bedroom. It landed on the wall and stuck there like a big glob of glue. I watched it slowly creep down the wall, one snot strand after another."

"I'm trying to eat," said Wilmer, fiddling with his creamed spinach.

"But that wasn't the best part. We ate meat-balls for dinner, and one got stuck in my throat and I started wheezing. My mom had to slap my back to get it out, and then it exploded in a giant ball of orange slime. It was like a volcano spewing lava all over the table. Is that awesome or what?"

"Er, what?" Wilmer guessed.

"And then you'll never believe what I burped up last night after dessert. I was watching TV and . . ."

Wilmer nodded, not listening. He stared across the lunchroom, four tables over, at the vibrant electric pink Roxie. She had coordinated her clothes to match, wearing socks, a T-shirt, and even a hair ribbon the exact same shade as her fuchsia hair.

But Wilmer wasn't the only one paying attention to her. She and her friends chatted with tall, handsome dodgeball star Zane Bradley. Roxie laughed, her big eyes crinkling in the corners, her pink lips melding into her pink face. It was hard to see where the lips stopped and her face began. Zane said something that was apparently so amusing that Roxie, Vonda, and Claire broke out in hysterical laughter. Wilmer's stomach growled with jealousy. He couldn't image Zane saying anything clever; Zane had always seemed somewhat of a thickheaded ignoramus: all brawn, no brain. Besides, Zane's lime green head clashed horribly with Roxie's pinkish hue.

Roxie stood up and walked with Zane to the dessert counter. She flashed him a small, shy smile. Her hand grazed his, maybe accidentally, but maybe not. Zane picked out a strawberry FrozenBUZZZZ! from the glass freezer case, its frozen rose shell almost the exact same color as Roxie's bright rosy eyes. Wilmer felt like he was being stabbed in the gut by his own father's ice-cream stick. Zane's and Roxie's hands brushed each other again. It was subtle and quick, but it rubbed against Wilmer like sandpaper.

Wilmer slowly chewed his spinach, but he tasted nothing except the sad, disturbing flavor of romantic failure.

"Can you believe it?" shouted Ernie. Wilmer had forgotten Ernie was still talking. And bouncing. "A three-foot orange spitball!"

"Right. Sure. Uh-huh," said Wilmer.

"Hey! Want to race to the gym and back?"

"Not really. I'm eating. Was eating. Maybe eating." He slid his plate away. He had lost his appetite, not from Ernie's sickening stories, but from Zane Bradley's arrogant, Roxie-aimed grin.

Ernie smiled and bounced.

II.

Ernie and Wilmer headed back to class. Wilmer slowly shuffled, and Ernie skipped, hopped, and cartwheeled. Wilmer had to admit that Ernie performed pretty decent cartwheels. Wilmer felt like he was in slow motion amid the blur of kids bouncing and dashing about like randomly zinged rubber bands. He estimated the class was approximately 114 percent more active than usual.

Then the PA system crackled, followed by a long squeal that pierced through Wilmer's ears like an off-key vuvuzela. A moment later the equally off-key and jarring voice of Principal Shropshire sliced through the hallway.

"Excuse me. Ahem. Is this thing on?" he began. "Ahem. Yes. So. As many of you have noticed, some of our sixth graders who are not normally very bright have become so." After a pause the principal cleared his throat again. "Ahem. That's, um, not to say they are not normally bright, as in smart, and they've suddenly become bright, as in smart, because they haven't. I mean, they already are. Smart, that is. Some, at least. You know who you are, the smart ones. But in this case I refer to their hue. They are brightly colored. I hope that clears up any confusion."

Wilmer's already sunken heart sank even further into his gut. School was about to be canceled, he was sure of it, and as a result so would Wilmer's chances for the Sixth-Grade Science Medal. He wouldn't be able to observe, take samples, and solve the mystery. Even worse, his chance to win Roxie's heart might be tossed away like week-old cabbage, or perhaps like three-week-old cabbage, such as that in Mrs. Dooley's frightening fish-oil-lathered three-week-old cabbage soufflé side dish from last Thursday's dinner.

The PA system squealed again as Principal Shropshire cleared his throat. "Sorry. Ahem. As I was saying, our sixth-grade students are quite bright, as in colorful. I have met with the school board. Well, not actually met with them, but I've talked over the phone with them. That sort of counts as meeting them, does it not? Um, maybe. Anyway, we've decided that due to the rapidly spreading nature of this disease, combined with the ability of our students to continue functioning perfectly well under the circumstances, all those who are sick should *stay* in school. I will send a letter home with each of you tonight, giving your parents the option of keeping their healthy children home. If there are any left. So, again, sick means school. Healthy students can leave. Or stay. Yes, that's all. Thank you. Ahem."

The PA system screeched again, and then the hallway was bathed in silence.

Followed immediately by an eruption of cheers.

"Why would anyone want to stay home?" screamed Cody Bimble.

"It's just starting to get interesting!" yelled Jason Mertz.

"Let's play leapfrog!" shouted Charlie Chen.

"Yippee!" hollered Ernie, slapping Wilmer's back and planting a big green kiss on the surprised Claire Huddleston's lavender-hued mouth. A green streak lingered on her lips. She screamed and covered her face with her hands and ran back to Roxie and Vonda, who were high-fiving along with the rest of the class.

Wilmer was delighted too. Now he could stay and solve this medical enigma. Even though he was healthy, his parents wouldn't object to him attending. They hadn't even noticed Sherman's aquamarine head last night.

Wilmer would solve this case. He knew he could! After all, no one could crack scientific conundrums as well as Wilmer Dooley, the greatest sixth-grade scientist in school.

Down the hall Roxie and Zane exchanged fist bumps.

Wilmer sighed. Science was so much easier to understand than girls.

III.

That night, Wilmer sat next to a now scarlet and yellow Sherman at the dinner table, frustrated at his lack of ideas. If food was the cause of the contagion, why was Wilmer the same ho-hum color as always? If food—what food? Or was it lots of foods combined?

As usual, supper was an adventure of odd flavors. Was that cumin in the cucumber mash, with a hint of sesame seed oil and lime juice? There was one unidentifiable ingredient, maybe shoe polish, that left Wilmer's teeth slightly blackened. After eating, Mr. Dooley went back down to the basement, eager to continue his secret experiments, which he promised would "change everything!" Wilmer doubted this statement was true, since if it changed *everything*, that would include language, body functions, planets, the law of gravity, rainbows, his socks, and the smell of puppy dogs—and he severely doubted his father was working on anything that far reaching.

Still, Wilmer was intrigued. His father wasn't normally so secretive. Usually he absentmindedly let crucial details about his work slip out. But this time he was as mum as a mummy. Whatever Mr. Dooley was dabbling with downstairs, it was big.

As Wilmer sat lost in thought, Sherman grumbled in his chair. He picked up the tall glass

of sapphire-colored Blueberry MilkBUZZZZ! that Mrs. Dooley had poured him for dessert, but then put it back down, untouched. Mrs. Dooley had gently scolded him earlier in the meal, telling him to "try not to be so multicolored at the dinner table, dear." Sherman had taken the reprimand a bit too personally.

Sherman wasn't normally one to skip dessert, but he did tonight. He pushed his chair away and began sprinting around the table.

"Don't you get dizzy?" asked Wilmer, amazed at Sherman's constant stream of energy.

"I'm sweating my yellow out," said Sherman, racing. "Maybe I can sweat orange instead. Orange is way cooler than yellow."

Wilmer shrugged. He didn't think yellow or orange was particularly cool. Solving scientific questions—now, *that* was cool.

Preston reached over from his high chair and grabbed the tall glass of Blueberry MilkBUZZZZ! He slurped a taste. He splashed the drink in his mouth. His ears twitched, and then a moment later he spit it back out on the table. "Yuck!" he wailed.

Wilmer didn't blame him; he couldn't understand how Sherman, or any of the kids at school, could swallow that junk.

Wilmer stared at the thick, large glass of glowing blue milk. Traces of Sherman's grubby, colorful fingerprints remained on its surface. In those fingerprints Sherman's DNA strands lingered, perhaps glowing as radiantly as they did on Sherman.

Observation!

That was exactly what Wilmer needed. More samples. More DNA. His classmates were a walking cesspool of infectious germs. He needed to find willing guinea pigs, living samples oozing color and ripe for experimentation.

Tomorrow would be a new day. As soon as he arrived in school, Wilmer would begin collecting specimens as quickly as possible.

After all the observation Wilmer was about to do, there was no possible way this perplexing pretzel would stay twisted.

TUESDAY
Day 8

Dear Journal,

   A science experiment is only as valuable as its specimens. For example, last month I attempted to discover a link between brain size and muscle mass. That is to say, the larger the muscles, the smaller the brain. To prove my theory, I needed to acquire a cranium sample from Zane Bradley (big muscles, small brain) to compare with my own (big brain, muscles . . . not so big). Unfortunately, my repeated attempts at inserting tweezers into Zane's ear to collect bits of his brain were unsuccessful. He threatened to detach my nose from my face if I came near him again. I'm fond of my nose. I use it often.

   Needless to say, my experiment remains unfinished.

   But right now I have bigger concerns than muscle-to-brain ratios. You guessed it, Journal—the epidemic.

School was packed this morning; kids who had stayed home sick yesterday were back, likely because of Principal Shropshire's letter. Kids in the school yard were perkier, too. Dozens played a particularly enthusiastic game of tag, in which it appeared that everyone was It at the same time. Ernie begged me to play, but I don't think I could have kept up with everyone. Other kids engaged in a complicated game of Twister that three teachers eventually had to help unscramble. A large gathering of girls performed an impressive chorus line, and a crew of redheaded girls (and four orange-headed ones) began Irish step-dancing.

I researched hyperactive diseases and came across something called restless legs syndrome. That disorder often gives people the urge to walk, stretch, bike, do yoga, and other things. But I don't think anyone's ever felt compelled to do push-ups, run twelve miles, and then pogo-stick to school like Susie Pepperton says she did this morning. She didn't even seem tired, although, oddly, she insisted the pogo-sticking was her legs' idea and not hers.

The colors have mutated too. Rather than just a

single hue, now many kids are sporting patterns, such as a plaid Mandy Wilkerson and a paisley Elvira Menkin. Poor Jeremy Lange's red-and-white-striped face looks almost exactly like a barbershop pole.

But my sample taking is off to an impressive start. I set up a small table behind the bleachers and posted a handwritten sign: BECOME A PART OF MEDICAL HISTORY! CONTRIBUTE TO THE CURE! DONATE YOUR SPIT TODAY!

By the time the school bell rang, I had collected two dozen plastic cups filled with brightly glowing saliva, from Felix Frostmire's chartreuse-stained slobber to Eric Eckersly's indigo drool.

Business started slowly but became brisk after I announced I was giving away free packets of Sugar-BUZZZZ! with every donated sample. Good thing I grabbed a few handfuls from our lifetime stash under the stairs. Most kids ripped open their packet and downed it right there at my table and then dashed away to perform backflips and handsprings. In the case of scarlet-spotted sixth-grade gymnastics champion Sara Stapps, she celebrated her free packet with an impressive one-handed round-off. It might have scored a perfect ten if she had performed in front of a panel of floor-exercise judges.

Roxie donated her saliva too. She even spits gloriously. She held her cup, her lips pursing elegantly before gently blowing out a small bright pink stream of liquid. I'm tempted to keep the sample as a souvenir rather than use it for testing. But then again, that's sort of weird.

I carefully marked the time and date on each cup before sliding them into insulated shoe boxes to bring home later. As first period neared, I started to clean up and noticed Claudius Dill watching me. I can't prove he's planning something. That would be pure guesswork and not scientific certainty. But science is also about gut instinct, and my gut tells me to be careful.

But not even Claudius can stop me from solving this mystery. The solution will be mine, along with the science award and maybe even Roxie's eternal gratitude. I'm not sure which I want more.

Signing off,
Wilmer Dooley

I.

Wilmer was excited to begin experimenting with his three large shoe boxes of samples. At lunch he quickly gobbled his spinach. He convinced Ernie to follow him to the biology lab.

"Do I have to play lookout while you're in the lab *again*?" complained Ernie, bouncing down the hall. "I'd rather run wind sprints. Seriously. Want to race me, please? Please? Pretty please? Pretty, pretty please? Please, please, please, please, please?" Even his pleading bounced everywhere.

"Sorry. I need to solve this, Ernie. I only need a few minutes, and I don't want Mrs. Padgett walking in. You know how she gets. Do you remember the warning signal?"

"I hoot like an owl. Three hoots and Mrs. Padgett is coming. Two hoots and it's Principal Shropshire. One hoot and a student is coming. But I really don't give a hoot."

"You have to give a hoot. That's the signal."

"But there aren't owls in the school. Why don't I just knock on the door if someone is coming?"

Wilmer nodded. "Even better. See? You're a

natural guard. Now stay here. You can do sit-ups or something."

"Great!" said Ernie, getting down on the floor and quickly crunching his stomach.

Wilmer closed the door and removed three cups of spit from the first shoe box. He had also swiped a number of materials from the cafeteria to test. He dipped a small forkful of meat loaf puree into a green glowing cup and waited. Nothing happened. He quickly jotted down the disappointing results in his notebook.

Wilmer plopped a small spoonful of melted Strawberry Shortcake IceeBUZZZZ! into the next spit sample. Immediately the cup bubbled and glowed! Excited, he added some Broccoli-Cabbage Surprise to the mix.

The glow faded, but only slightly. Wilmer added the development to his records and continued jotting down results from his other tests:

- Lemon-Lime PuddingBUZZZZ! glows
  and burps one giant bubble glop before
  resting comfortably.

- Soggy sloppy joe bun dims glow by 37 percent, estimated.
- Limp green bean casserole increases gleam by 4.3 percent and then reduces it by 9.6 percent, for a net loss of 5.3 percent.

He was definitely on to something! He felt a sharp buzz of scientific excitement race through his neck.

The feeling was replaced with concern when Wilmer heard noises from outside the door. The sounds were muffled, so he wasn't exactly sure who was speaking, but he didn't hear any knocking or owl hooting. So he continued mixing, but cautiously, on the alert for intruders.

II.

Valveeta Padgett stuck her head down the hallway. What was Ernie Rinehart doing outside her room? She didn't like to see kids lingering by her door when they were supposed to be somewhere else, such as the lunchroom, and she knew Ernie was seldom far from Wilmer Dooley. Ernie was doing sit-ups, annoyingly oozing energy like so many other kids this week. A trio of girls walked past. Mrs. Padgett recognized Roxie McGhee's pink face, followed by Vonda Binkowski and Claire Huddleston, orange and lavender, respectively.

"Have you seen Carly Trundle?" said Vonda. "One side of her face is blue. One side is red. And the middle is yellow. She looks like a rainbow snow cone."

"That's nothing," said Claire. "The top of Billy Bobcott's head is red. The middle is white, and his chin is blue. They're calling him Billy Bomb Pop!"

Mrs. Padgett watched Ernie follow the girls down the hall, singing and twirling his arms in what might have been an attempt at Bollywood dancing. Mrs. Padgett recognized the tune: "My Bonnie Lies over the Ocean." But instead Ernie sang, "My boogers lie over the ocean." He accompanied his tune with some fancy nose blowing of green nasal discharge.

Whether it was an unsuccessful attempt at humor or Ernie had forgotten the proper words,

Mrs. Padgett couldn't say for sure, but she took the opportunity to head to the door of her now unblocked room. She peered through the small glass window.

Just as she suspected, Wilmer was inside, fiddling around with her things. She debated rushing in and surprising him. Instead she watched, intrigued. What was he up to? Maybe something for his Sixth-Grade Science Medal entry? Unfortunately, she couldn't see very well. Wilmer's back was to her. He wasn't jigging. But he seemed to be mixing things in test tubes. Test tubes! What if they were from her missing fourteen? That would be all the proof she would need that he was a thief, a liar, and other unpleasant words that she would think of on the way to the principal's office.

A ragamuffin. That was another good word she could use.

Excited, she leaped off the ground in joy, but when she landed, the heel of her shoe snapped in half and she found herself in an awkward position of half standing and half falling, flailing her arms to balance herself. Then the falling half took control, and she crumbled to the ground.

Luckily, no one saw her. She was embarrassed but not injured.

As she struggled to her feet, wiping dust from her black skirt, she heard someone singing "Row, Row, Row Your Boat." No. These lyrics were "Blow, blow, blow your nose," followed by giggles and shouts of "You are just *gross*, Ernie!"

Mrs. Padgett hurried away. She still wasn't sure what Wilmer was doing, but she was convinced it had something to do with this strange illness. If he made any interesting discoveries, she might be forced to consider giving him the Sixth-Grade Science Medal. Never! It was time to call in the experts. She took her phone from her pocket to call the office of Dr. Fernando Dill, the World's Greatest Doctor.

III.

What was that? Wilmer heard a thud outside the door, as if someone had fallen. Maybe it was Ernie signaling. He was supposed to hoot like an owl or knock, not thud. Still, it was some sort of signal, Wilmer was sure of it. He quickly crammed the test tubes into his backpack, along with his unused samples. He would examine these more closely at home. But how? He wasn't allowed into his dad's lab. Wilmer paused for a moment before stuffing one of the lab microscopes into his backpack. He muttered a quick vow to the Gods of the Science Lab that he would return it safely and quickly, if only no one caught him.

The door swung open, and Ernie stood in the doorway holding a tissue filled with green, flowing snot.

"Anyone coming?" asked Wilmer.

"Nope. It's been quiet as a caterpillar. But we should get going. Class is going to start soon."

Wilmer nodded and grabbed his now very heavy backpack. Ernie hummed to himself as they walked, but Wilmer couldn't quite place the tune. "My Bonnie Lies over the Ocean"? Maybe.

IV.

An ultramarine-and-gold-striped Sherman raced around the kitchen table that evening, pausing only briefly to sneeze bright rainbow slime from his nose. Sherman kept yelling, "Giddyup! Giddyup!"

in a pathetic fake-Western drawl. Wilmer had to admit, Sherman had the worst case of the Mumpley plague he had seen yet.

But that was fortunate for Wilmer. He had the best test subject of all—right in his very house!

"Sherman. Stop running. I need you to come upstairs and be a guinea pig."

"I can be one right here." Sherman oinked and snorted, but he didn't stop running, except to sneeze.

"Not a pig. A guinea pig."

"Do they oink?"

"I don't think so. I need to do some tests on you. Do you want to be brightly colored your whole life?"

"Sure!" said Sherman, sneezing again.

"Don't you want to be cured?" asked Wilmer.

"No. Why?"

"Because you're sneezing everywhere?"

Sherman held up his hand. It blinked red and yellow. "But I'm also doing this. Isn't that awesome?" Sneeze.

"It's certainly curious. Come on. I just need you to eat stuff."

If there was anything Sherman liked more than running around in circles, it was eating stuff. "Okay," he said, and sneezed a large drop of pinkish goop. "But you better have a lot to eat! I'll race you upstairs!"

Wilmer shook his head. Sherman's hyper energy level seemed to have increased, and that was saying a lot. As Wilmer headed toward the staircase, the front door opened and Mrs. Dooley walked in. She held an empty pot, which she often used to water the vegetables in her garden outside. Crusts of dirt clung to her cheeks and arms.

"Hi, Mom," said Wilmer. "Sherman and I will be upstairs doing experiments to see why he's changing colors."

Mrs. Dooley sighed. "It's just because he has a vivid imagination. Anyone can see that."

Wilmer blinked. "Mom, he's flashing like a disco ball."

She shrugged. "Back when I was younger, we liked disco. But you two go up and listen to whatever music your generation prefers."

Wilmer sighed and headed upstairs. Both his

parents prided themselves on observation. But both seemed to be blind to the colorful changes happening in their very house. Wilmer supposed it was for the best. It made it that much easier for him to conduct his own research. He wanted to solve this mystery alone.

Wilmer shut his bedroom door behind them. Sherman ran in circles. Since Wilmer didn't have a lot of floor space, Sherman had to run in very small circles. It was really more spinning than running. Meanwhile, Wilmer set up his stolen—or rather, borrowed—microscope and removed the test tubes from his backpack.

Wilmer opened the first test tube, filled with a combination of string beans and meat loaf gravy. Sherman stopped running only long enough to grab it from Wilmer's hand and chug it down with one gulp. "Not bad!" he shouted.

Sherman's neck flickered a drab olive color three times and then stopped.

Wilmer strapped on his dad's old research goggles (scientists often wear goggles), tapped the small beaker in his pocket (scientists always use beakers), and then scribbled a few words in his notebook. He handed Sherman the next test tube. This one was filled with a few tablespoons of PuddingBUZZZZ! mixed with granola and iced tea. Sherman grabbed it and swallowed.

Sherman coughed, and his left ear turned coral pink.

Sherman sneezed, and his right ear turned turquoise.

Sherman hiccupped, and both ears turned vermilion.

Interesting! Spellbinding! Odd! Wilmer wrote these results into his scientific journal and handed Sherman the next test tube. This one was filled with the melted IceeBUZZZZ!

Sherman took it, swallowed, and rubbed his stomach. "Delicious!" he cried.

It was as if a laser light show exploded in Sherman's head. Bright neon green and auburn lights flashed on his forehead, cheek, and nose. Ocean-blue-colored blobs erupted on his chin and ears. His neck lit up in a swirling kaleidoscope of goldenrod and tangerine. Sherman's eyes rolled in circles, his pupils flashing cyan before quickly returning to their natural black color.

"I love when that happens!" cried Sherman, jumping up and down. "Can we do it again?"

Wilmer wrote frantically in his notebook.

Sherman spun in circles again, this time with the artistic grace and speed of an Olympic ice-skater. Wilmer grew dizzy just watching him.

Ten test tubes later Wilmer studied his notes carefully. The most sugary treats had the greatest side effects, while a sprig of parsley did nothing but make Sherman scratch his elbow. When they were done, Sherman sprinted out of the room and back down the stairs. Wilmer lay down on his bed to think.

Within minutes Mrs. Dooley shouted, "Dinner-time!" Wilmer tromped downstairs and sat down at the kitchen table. He just barely sidestepped the racing Sherman, who yelped loudly while his rainbow face blinked. "Get along, little dogie!" he cried. Mrs. Dooley didn't pay attention to him, as if yelping, blinking rainbow boys were as common as house ants. Besides, she was busy putting the finishing touches on the night's Hawaiian Baked Bean–Sushi Surprise. (Preston suggested it needed a pinch of curry powder and one olive.)

Just as Mrs. Dooley finished plopping generous dinner portions on each plate, Mr. Dooley finally emerged from his laboratory. His hair stood straight up, and he wore bright orange goggles on his head.

"I'm getting close," he declared excitedly. "My invention will forever transform the way kids eat!"

"That's nice, dear," said Mrs. Dooley. "You shouldn't wear your goggles at the dinner table."

"Quite right," agreed Mr. Dooley, sinking down in his chair. "All this work has made me famished!"

"What's the invention, Dad?" asked Wilmer.

"A scientist never tells until he's ready," said Mr. Dooley.

Despite his curiosity, Wilmer knew better than to ask for details. Besides, he had his own science experiments to think about.

WEDNESDAY
Day 9

Dear Journal,

Sometimes scientific advancement happens suddenly and without warning, like when an apple drops from a tree and you discover gravity. Or when a watermelon slice falls on your lap and you invent napkins. Other times it happens slowly. As I reported earlier, it took more than four hundred years to find what caused the Black Death. But the Sixth-Grade Science Medal will be awarded in less than four weeks, not in four hundred years.

I need to solve this puzzle now. But I'm far from any real answers. And attendance at my spit booth was disappointing today. I received a puce-colored saliva sample from Bern Whirley, but he gave me a cupful yesterday, too. He grabbed his free Sugar-BUZZZZ! pack, downed it in one gulp, and then

sprinted off to climb a tree upside down. He made it look much easier than you'd think.

Elvira Menkin almost stopped by too. But it was like she couldn't get her legs to stand still. She yelped, "Hold on! . . . Wait a second. . . . Hello again. . . . Now I'm stopping. . . . Nope, maybe now . . . ," as she raced back and forth past me twelve times and then ran off.

Finally, with no one else stopping by to supply spit, I packed up early.

But I have observed a significant shift in mood. I overheard Gabi Lersh tell Bella Bimms that she wished she had never turned pumpkin. Bella replied she was equally tired of her bright apricot head. Then they both did backflips, but without enthusiasm.

I overheard plenty of other kids grumble. A tie-dyed Caleb Koolidge moonwalked past me, yelling, "I hate dancing! Make it stop!" Then he did the Robot, followed by the Hustle.

Kids want to be cured.

Some of the older kids are showing symptoms too. Gary Grumbel, a seventh-grade bully who is

fond of stealing sixth-grader lunches, has a particularly nasty case of peppermint stripes. I can't
say I'm sorry about that.

Even Claudius Dill, who had previously been
untouched by the disease, has been stricken.
He showed up this morning with a horrible case of
electrifying indigo and kelly green zigzags. At one
point he sneezed, and I think I saw him smirk. If
so, he might be the only kid in school happy he has
the bug.

I'm the only student left in the sixth-grade
wing who doesn't have a case of these contagious
colors. No wonder Roxie barely notices me. It's hard
to stand out when you have boring, bland skin and
everyone else looks like they lost a fight with a
paint factory.

While I packed up my table, Zane Bradley talked
to Roxie. She smiled. He laughed. I felt sick. I still
think his lime green face clashes with her perfectly
tinted pink. What does she see in him, anyway?
Other than muscles and dashing good looks, I mean.

No epidemic infects every person in its reach;
some people are immune. Hundreds of years ago

not everyone in Europe caught the bubonic plague. If I can figure out why I'm not infected, maybe I can find a cure. It's my best chance at beating this bacteria.

Signing off,
Wilmer Dooley

I.

Claudius Dill sneezed as loudly and as terribly as he could muster. He had practiced sneezing all morning in front of a mirror. He didn't want merely to sneeze, after all. He needed to have the grossest, biggest, and most ear-splattering sneezes in school.

After 116 practice sneezes he was ready.

"Why are you sneezing so much, dear?" asked Mrs. Dill. But when Claudius stepped out of the bathroom and his mother saw the bright colors covering every inch of her son, her mouth gaped open. "Oh, Claudius!" she moaned. "You too?"

One hour later Claudius stood in the school yard waiting for the bell to ring. His bright purplish zigzags gleamed. He sneezed so loudly that three kids turned around to look.

"Wow, Claudius. You have it bad, huh?" said Tommy Dorps, staring at Claudius with his yellow-striped face.

"Caught it last night!" yelled Claudius. "I'm coughing and sneezing a lot!" Five other students turned to look. "Sorry! My ears are clogged!" Claudius explained, shouting.

"You look very zigzaggy today," exclaimed Mandy Wilkerson. "I hate my green and blue argyle. It clashes with half my wardrobe. What do you think?" She pointed to her orange T-shirt.

But Claudius didn't answer. Instead he coughed and sneezed on Mandy's face. "Sorry," said Claudius, sneezing one more time for good measure.

Mandy wiped her face and walked away as Claudius grinned to himself. Under his shirt, hidden from view, he wore his EVIL GENIUS T-shirt. It seemed fitting for today. Catching the disease was only the first step in his plan.

It was time to stop simply wearing his EVIL GENIUS shirt; it was time to start living the life!

Money didn't grow on trees, but it might soon be lining Claudius's pockets. Along with a new, shiny Sixth-Grade Science Medal.

"Excuse me, Claudius Dill?" Roxie McGhee waved as she approached. What did she want? She clutched a notepad and had a pencil tucked behind her ear. She was so vibrantly pink she was almost blinding! Claudius shielded his eyes, wishing for sunglasses. "As you probably know, I'm a reporter for *Mumpley Musings*. I'm doing a report on the epidemic. You've got the worst case I've seen."

"Thank you," said Claudius, who then coughed. He almost sneezed on Roxie but decided to wait.

"When did you first catch it?"

"Just this morning. I was in the bathroom, and when I walked out, I looked like this." Claudius stifled an evil grin.

"Some students are scared they might be multicolored forever. What do you think?"

"Oh, I don't know. By the end of the day kids might feel a little differently about that."

"What do you mean?" asked Roxie, frantically scribbling notes.

"Oh, nothing," said Claudius.

"But you said—"

A well-placed sneeze into Roxie's face ended that line of questioning. "Sorry." Claudius turned away and coughed to disguise the laugh that was about to trickle out of the side of his mouth.

II.

During study hall Wilmer sat in the back of the class, desperately trying to concentrate on algebra. But his mind kept diving into contagious colored waters. His schoolwork was starting to suffer—how could he concentrate when there was so much to observe? Kids twitched in their chairs; even when sitting, they were never completely motionless. A couple of classmates waved their arms wildly, seemingly out of control. Twice, Wilmer had to duck or be swatted on the nose. Only Wilmer and, oddly, Claudius, were still. Wilmer made a note that Claudius didn't seem as energetic as the other kids. He seemed almost sluggish. Maybe he had a different strain of the sickness?

Bacteria are like that. They change and morph

and twist, so that eventually, instead of needing to find one cure, you need to find a dozen of them. Wilmer needed to solve this mystery sooner rather than later. It would be almost impossible to stop the pathogen if it mutated into a new, maybe even worse, strain.

Mr. Snellsny, the study hall teacher, stood up from behind his desk and cleared his throat. He was a small wisp of a man, with only a few strands of hair, but he combed each of them carefully throughout the day. "Excuse me. Class. Hello?" He patted his hair strands. "I need to make a phone call. Please continue to study and twitch in your seats." He stepped out and closed the door behind him.

No sooner had the door clicked shut than Claudius Dill jumped out of his seat and ran to the front of the room. He bounded up onto Mr. Snellsny's desk. The class looked at him, surprised. Claudius Dill wasn't normally the type to leap onto teachers' desks. Perhaps the disease was making him more active after all.

"Students of Mumpley Middle School!" he announced loudly, his left hand in his pocket, his other holding a small plastic cup filled with a glowing and murky greenish liquid. "I, Claudius Dill, the School's Greatest Scientist"—he looked directly at Wilmer when he said that, his mouth curled as if gloating—"have found the cure for the Mumpley plague! Watch me now as I try a dose in this very study hall! Then find me by my locker after class. And prepare to be amazed!" Claudius lifted the cup, thrust it forward as if offering a toast, and then downed the medicine in one mighty gulp. The class leaned forward in anticipation. "I think it's doing something," said Claudius. "I feel the miraculous effects of this wonder cure gurgling inside me! Wait! . . . I . . ." He lifted his left hand, the one that had been hidden inside his pocket since he first stood up.

The bright color was gone! He held his hand high in the air, comparing it with his other, zigzagged one. "It's working!" he cried. He threw down the cup, thrust both his fists up in triumph, and dashed out of the room.

The class was completely silent. Stunned.

Mr. Snellsny returned to the room. He didn't

notice Claudius missing. He sat in his seat and nodded, apparently happy the class was so quiet in his absence. But the silence in the room was quickly replaced with antsy muttering.

"Do you think it's true?" whispered Mason Allbright.

"His hand was completely color-free!" said Felix Frostmire.

"Sshhh!" said Mr. Snellsny.

Wilmer sat back, fuming. Claudius had found a cure? How was that possible? Wilmer had been working nonstop, and he wasn't even close. Wilmer was the greatest sixth-grade scientist at Mumpley Middle School, *not* Claudius Dill. Claudius was nothing but a charlatan! A fake! Wilmer was convinced that when all the kids found Claudius after class, he would still be zigzagged.

But what if he wasn't?

Class ended in five minutes. The schoolroom clock ticked slower than usual. Wilmer kept glancing at it, surprised that only a few seconds had passed since the last time he looked. He wondered if time ticked slower when you wanted it to move faster. It would be a worthwhile experiment, although difficult to perform, since the very act of looking forward to an experiment might slow down time by itself. Wilmer was thinking that using a stopwatch in a vacuum might eliminate the time-over-matter dilemma, which would then isolate the passage of time conductivity, when the bell rang and all twenty-three students jumped out of their seats and rushed to the door.

III.

Wilmer waited until the crush of kids pushed through the door frame, and then he followed behind. Somehow word of Claudius's transformation had spread through the entire sixth-grade wing. A large surge of kids descended on Claudius's locker. Every inch of available space was filled, with kids in the back craning their necks to get a better look, many jogging in place, unable to keep their legs still. Claudius must have brought a chair to stand on, because a moment later his face towered over the crowd.

His completely nonzigzaggy face.

Claudius's head might have been wet and flushed and red, as if it had been rubbed roughly, but it was otherwise back to its normal color. There was no denying that.

The crowd gasped. Wilmer's mouth fell open like a torn bag of potato chips. Close by, Roxie frantically scribbled notes into her reporter notepad. Claire and Vonda both clapped in excitement.

"As you can see, I'm cured!" shouted Claudius. The crowd erupted in hoots and delighted whoops. Three tangerine-colored girls began shouting, "Claudius! Claudius!" and a hundred kids joined in. Claudius lowered his hands for them to quiet down. He wanted to speak. "My cure is complete, and I want to share it with each of you! For free!"

Shouts of "Hurray!" filled the hallway until, once again, Claudius motioned for everyone to be silent. "But while I *want* to give it to you for free, I'm afraid I can't. It's just too expensive. So I'm happy to offer Claudius's Colorful Contagion Cure right now, for the small, nominal price of nine ninety-nine a dose."

Wilmer knew you should never cry "Fire!" in

a crowded movie house. You should also never cry "Movie!" in a crowded firehouse, as it would likely be untrue. But neither shout could ever have caused the frenzied rush that Claudius's announcement created. Waves of kids rocked forward, wiggling ten-dollar bills over their heads as they competed to be the first to grab the Claudius Cure.

Wilmer stayed where he was, still barely believing what he saw. Soon kids sprinted past him holding their coveted small milk cartons now filled with Claudius's murky green medicine. Those lucky enough to have bought the contagion cure cradled their containers as if they were valuable diamonds or gems.

Some downed the cure and immediately declared they felt better, although their color didn't fade and their jitters didn't cease. But these proclamations made the crowd surge tighter around Claudius's locker.

"One at a time!" Claudius shouted from within the teeming masses. "Please have your money ready."

Wilmer shook his head, bewildered. How had

Claudius done it, when Wilmer hadn't? Maybe Wilmer wasn't the greatest sixth-grade scientist at school. Maybe he had been wrong about Claudius.

Wilmer had zero chance of winning that Sixth-Grade Science Medal now.

And he had a less than zero chance of winning Roxie's heart.

Ten minutes later the halls emptied as more and more kids ran off with their new purchases. "Sorry, all out! I'll bring a new batch tomorrow!" screamed Claudius. There was a group moan from those still in line.

"I'll give you twenty dollars for your cure!" said Billy Bobcott to Jeremy Lange as they pushed past Wilmer.

"No way," said Jeremy.

"Fifty dollars!" screamed Billy, but other kids littering the hallway swallowed them up before Wilmer could hear Jeremy's response. Kids without cures quickly surrounded those who had them, bidding against one another for a taste.

Wilmer's face turned red, and not from any

contagion. It must be a trick. That was the only explanation! Fuming, he pushed past a throng of kids offering all their money for Bern Whirley's carton of cure.

IV.

Mrs. Padgett watched the commotion from the end of the hallway. She considered rushing over and breaking up the large flock of students gathered in a circle. Selling medicine in school was against 334 school rules. But then she held back. Was that really Claudius? Had that boy actually found a cure on his own?

Mrs. Padgett had received a voice mail that very morning. She replayed the recording from her memory.

"Mrs. Padgett? This is Dr. Dill returning your call. This calamitous contagion is intriguing. I'm in Indonesia for a measles conference but will get right on this problem when I'm free, whenever that is. I'm confident I can find a cure within the next year or two. Good-bye, or as they say in Indonesia: *Selamat tinggal!*"

Mrs. Padgett had been disappointed by the message. She didn't have months to wait, or years. But now her disappointment warped into surprised delight.

Still, Valveeta Padgett was skeptical. Claudius Dill was a suck-up but not the brightest bulb on the chandelier. That was one of the reasons she liked him; he was no threat to her intellect. Her small smile widened when she saw Wilmer watching the commotion, clearly agitated. She hadn't quite developed a plan on how exactly to ensure that Claudius would win the Sixth-Grade Science Medal, but maybe she no longer needed to worry. Claudius might actually win it on his own merit now, however unlikely that seemed. Why, the boy would practically have been flunking biology if Mrs. Padgett hadn't been changing his test scores all year!

But Claudius cleaned whiteboards exceptionally well, and that counted for something. In her book, sucking up counted for quite a lot. She nodded in approval and turned on her heel just as Principal Shropshire approached. He waddled closer, his short legs carrying his large belly across the floor a bit faster than Mrs. Padgett would have thought possible.

"What is, um, going on?" he asked, pointing to the crowd and adjusting his thick, black-rimmed glasses. "Is there a fire? A hamster on the loose? Perhaps a troll? Not that we have trolls in our school, of course, but if we do, I want to know. I am principal, after all, and trolls are my responsibility. I'm pretty sure they are, at least. I'll need to check the school guidelines to make sure."

"There are no trolls, I assure you," said Mrs. Padgett. "Just kids having fun. By the way, have I shown you slides of the rare Mexican sleeping frog in my lab? Fascinating. They sleep with their eyes open but their ears closed. Let's hurry to my class and take a look." She needed to guide Principal Shropshire away so that Claudius would not get in trouble for selling his cure at school.

"Um, er, I do like frogs," said Principal Shropshire as he was led away. "But that crowd of kids . . ."

"Nothing to see, nothing to see," Mrs. Padgett repeated, taking him by the arm and escorting him down the hall. "Not nearly as fascinating as my sleeping frog."

"If you insist, I suppose," said Principal Shropshire as they rounded the corner.

V.

"Hey, Wilmer! Wait up!" shouted Ernie. Wilmer thumped down the hall in such a rage at Claudius's success that he barely heard his friend calling out. Ernie ran up to him. "Can you believe Claudius found a cure?"

"No. I can't. Can you?"

"Well, I guess so. Maybe. I mean, I don't know. It's surprising. But his zigzags are gone. Isn't that great? Thumbshake?" He held up his thumb, waiting for Wilmer to exchange their secret best-friend finger grab. But Wilmer just glared at it. Ernie lowered his digit.

Wilmer frowned. Even Ernie believed Claudius's story! Didn't he know it must be a trick? Where was his loyalty? Then he saw what Ernie was cradling in his hand, and his lips quivered with rage. Ernie held a milk carton.

"A carton of cure?" spat Wilmer. "You too, Ernie? You too?" Wilmer turned away as disgust filled his head.

"Wait! You got it all wrong!" shouted Ernie, reaching out to grab Wilmer's shoulder. Wilmer jerked his arm away and raced forward without looking back.

"But Wilmer! You don't understand!" screamed Ernie. "Wait! . . ." His voice trailed off as Wilmer hurdled himself out the school doors and into the bright spring afternoon. He stared straight ahead, refusing to acknowledge the excited squeals of his cure-carrying classmates.

VI.

"Don't leave the table just yet. I have a new dessert!" shouted Mrs. Dooley after clearing away the last plate of mushroom-inspired noodle goulash from the kitchen table that evening. Mr. Dooley sat back and patted his belly. He had been in a remarkably good mood all evening, humming happily throughout the meal. He still refused to share details of his basement experiment, but he promised he would explain it all "any day now."

"So, Wilmer. How goes the science project?" asked Mr. Dooley. "The medal will be announced soon. Surely you have observed."

"I have. But it's not going well at all, Dad," Wilmer admitted with a disgruntled sigh.

"Well, I'm sure you'll come through. You're a Dooley, and Dooleys always come through. Did I tell you the story of the time there was a world-wide shortage of castor oil? I decided to solve the problem using a can of mosquito repellent and a thimble."

Wilmer sat up, surprised. "Actually, Dad, no. You haven't told me that one."

"Oh. Too bad," said Mr. Dooley, who scratched his nose and didn't say another word.

Mrs. Dooley brought over her upside-down, right-side-up, cream-filled, banana-flavored coconut Bundt tart with cream cheese pudding. Wilmer wasn't sure why it burped twice. He pushed it away. Sherman, whose cheeks were busy flashing between deep carrot orange and cyan, dug into his bowl with great zeal. Preston gnawed on a chicken bone.

The television blared from the corner of the family room. Mrs. Dooley had turned it on so that she could watch her favorite cooking show, *Cooking on High*, which featured famous chefs preparing meals while wearing stilts. Wilmer didn't pay any attention to it until the deep baritone voice of local newscaster Guy Dimples rang out from the set.

"This is Guy Dimples. We interrupt this program to bring you a fascinating development on our local color contagion." Wilmer bolted upright and twisted his neck to view the screen in the other room. It was a good thing he'd skipped dessert, as he would likely have coughed it up on the table.

Because on the TV was none other than Claudius Dill.

Claudius sat on a green leather couch. He wore a plain red tie and a blue sport jacket. His hair was carefully combed. Across from him sat the blond and big-haired star reporter, Gwendolyn Bray. She shot Claudius a broad, perky smile.

"We are here with the boy who created a cure for the Mumpley malady, Claudius Dill. Claudius is the most brilliant scientist in the sixth grade. I heard you even saved your class iguana last semester."

Claudius nodded. "All in the day's work of a genius," he replied bashfully.

Wilmer bit his tongue. He could barely restrain himself from tackling the TV. He tromped into the family room to get a better look, his hands balled into tight, angry fists.

"Tell us," said Gwendolyn Bray, leaning closer, as if fascinated by every word streaming from Claudius's mouth. "How did you find a cure? I've heard our most renowned town doctors, including your own father, the respected, world-famous Dr. Fernando Dill, were stumped."

"He's just been busy. But I can't take all the credit. True, it was my brilliance that discovered the cure. True, it was my hard work that unstuck this sticky puzzle. True, it was my dedication that has made the difference for hundreds of kids. Well, come to think of it, I guess I can take all the credit."

Gwendolyn Bray laughed, as did Claudius. Wilmer's stomach flipped and lurched.

"But seriously. Everyone knows science is all

about genius. I suppose that's why I have the knack. And other people don't." It was as if Claudius had intended those words for Wilmer, and Wilmer alone. Claudius stared straight at the camera—straight at Wilmer.

"Science isn't about genius. It's about observation!" Wilmer shouted to the TV, disgusted, his face twisting with fury.

"What's that?" asked Mrs. Dooley. "Are you watching chefs on stilts? Has someone gotten a splinter?" Apparently, only Wilmer had been paying attention to the interview.

"No. Nothing," mumbled Wilmer.

"Everyone knows food tastes better when prepared on stilts," said Mrs. Dooley. She sighed. "I only wish I didn't have flat feet."

On TV, Claudius continued to stare into the camera. Wilmer again had the distinct impression that Claudius was staring directly at him. Claudius mumbled something.

"What was that?" asked Gwendolyn Bray.

"Nothing," said Claudius. "Nothing at all."

Wilmer's jaw dropped. He was convinced that

Claudius had just said, "This one's for Copernicus." But he couldn't be sure. Not really.

"Thank you, Claudius," said Gwendolyn. "It's an honor to speak to a real scientific hero." She turned to the camera and winked. "This is Gwendolyn Bray. And that's nothing but the truth!"

Wilmer slapped his forehead. He wanted to scream and scream and scream. He ran to the mud-room, slipped on some old boots, and rushed out the door and into the yard. He stomped and thumped his feet in a fit of uncontrollable rage. He whirled and twirled. It wasn't fair! It wasn't! He was so outraged that he didn't notice he was trampling his mom's vegetable garden, at least not until he had inflicted considerable damage on the turnips and an unfortunate tomato bush.

Finally, exhausted, he went back inside the house and upstairs to his room. He kicked off his dirty boots and lay on his bed. Outside, the sun was just beginning to set. A soft blue glow lit up his window, rising from the garden below.

Special Report

Special Report

Special Report

Special Report

THURSDAY
Day 10

Dear Journal,

There's a quote that great scientists recite time and time again: "The proof is in the pudding."

Maybe it's not exactly a scientific quote. But it is a quote. And a scientist must have said it at some point in time. After all, Albert Einstein loved tapioca pudding. He also loved ice-cream sundaes, but I don't know any science quotes about ice-cream sundaes.

Claudius's cure appears to be a complete failure. If anything, it's made things worse! The sixth-grade wing resembles a giant string of party lights. Colors flutter, twinkle, and swirl. Bella Bimms's star-spotted blinking earlobes were hard to miss when she briefly removed her earmuffs. No one understood why Charlie Chen was wearing a bandage over his nose, until the bandage fell off, revealing crimson and maize flashing stripes.

Kids are even more out of control too. They bounce off walls like heated gas molecules. They perform flips that would shame a circusful of acrobats. Many kids have deep bags under their eyes, like Sara Stapps. She says she hasn't slept in days, but instead spends her nights doing handstands.

You'd think this would discourage purchases of Claudius's ineffective cure, but you would be wrong. Claudius blames yesterday's lack of results on a faulty batch and claims his new and improved Claudius Cure will stop the epidemic in its tracks. He also says that his upgraded cure is a bit more expensive to make, and has upped the price to $14.67 a dose.

But kids don't seem to care. The line at his locker to buy old milk cartons filled with his murky green muck curves down the hallway. More kids are waiting than before—now infected seventh and eighth graders want the cure too.

I don't know what to think. Were Claudius's initial

results dumb luck? Is his cure a fake? But then, how did he cure himself?

"Trust me! Trust me! I've got it now!" I heard Claudius say to more than one customer.

But why anyone would trust Claudius Dill is beyond me.

Here's another outstanding quote: The great Sir Isaac Newton once said, "What we know is a drop; what we don't know is an ocean."

There's so much I don't know, I feel like I'm drowning.

Signing off,
Wilmer Dooley

I.

With mounting frustration, Wilmer watched the ever-expanding line trailing from Claudius Dill's locker. Claudius had become a celebrity overnight. Kids asked for his autograph. Quite a few took pictures of him. Couldn't they see that the epidemic was still spreading uncontrollably?

"What does Gwendolyn Bray eat?" asked Carly Trundle.

"Are you moving to Hollywood?" asked Felix Frostmire.

"Can I breathe the air you breathe?" asked Mandy Wilkerson, batting her dark green and navy blue plaid eyelids.

"Give me a break," snarled Wilmer under his breath, growing angrier and angrier.

Even Roxie was intrigued. She barraged Claudius with questions like "What did Gwendolyn Bray smell like?" and "Did she carry a reporter's journal like mine?"

Even though Wilmer hadn't caught the bug, he still felt sick to his stomach.

A turquoise and ruby diamond-patterned Susie Pepperton tapped Wilmer on the shoulder. "Did you take Claudius's cure?" she asked. "You're so lucky!"

Wilmer shook his head and snarled, "No. I haven't taken that medicine. If you were smart, you'd save your money. The cure doesn't work."

"It worked on you."

"I didn't catch the disease."

"I hope he doesn't sell out."

"It doesn't work!"

"I better get in line."

"It doesn't work!"

"You're so lucky to be cured by Claudius. He's my hero."

"I'm not cured!"

"He saved Copernicus last semester, you know."

"ARRGHHH!"

Susie ignored Wilmer's scream of anguish and rushed to stand in the back of the twisting, spreading crowd. Nearly everyone in school was waiting, including Roxie and her friends. Most found it impossible to stand still, so all throughout the line kids jumped, spun in circles, and flopped about. Some kids danced what looked to be the tango. Wilmer wanted to grab Roxie and pull her away, wrap her in his arms, and save her from whatever junk Claudius was peddling. And then, as long as she was in his arms, anyway, Wilmer would dance the tango with her too. Not that he could tango, but dancing was on his list of romantic-pursuit ideas he'd written down last week. Those days seemed long ago now.

Wilmer didn't dare to try that, though. He didn't dare even to talk to Roxie. She wouldn't listen to him, anyway. Why would she, when the entire school had fallen for Claudius's stupid and worthless rip-off of a cure?

Wilmer shook his head and turned from the crowd. He needed to get away before he exploded in frustration. As he turned, he spun smack into Ernie, who had been standing directly behind him.

"Watch where you're going!" snapped Wilmer.

"You ran into me!" protested Ernie, hopping in place, his bright green face now flashing like a broken traffic light.

"Well, you better get in line and get your stupid medicine. Not that it'll do you any good."

"Who says I want his medicine?" Ernie barked.

"I think we all know whose side you're on," hissed Wilmer.

"And whose side is that?"

"The wrong one, obviously," howled Wilmer, brushing past Ernie.

"I wanted to show you something!" cried Ernie. "But now I won't!"

As Wilmer stomped away, he passed Mrs. Padgett, who was vigorously arguing with Mr. Snellsny. "But the boy is doing no harm," she insisted.

"He's breaking about a million school rules!" yelped Mr. Snellsny, the four hairs on his head standing at attention.

"Surely you exaggerate. I bet you can't name just two."

"Conducting business in school. Dispensing medicine. Causing a disturbance."

"That's three rules, not two. I told you that you couldn't name just two."

"It needs to be stopped!" demanded Mr. Snellsny.

"Hogwash. The boy is a genius!"

"We are talking about the same boy, right?"

"Just give him a chance."

"Fine." Mr. Snellsny sighed, the air deflating from his chest. "I suppose you're right. Boys will be boys."

Wilmer continued walking. If even the teachers supported Claudius, what hope did Wilmer have of convincing anyone? His best friend was a traitor. The teachers were against him. He had never before felt so alone or frustrated.

"All sold out! Sorry!" shouted Claudius from down the hall. "Come back next week!" A collective groan spread across the hallway from legions of disappointed students.

Wilmer shook his head, dismayed.

II.

Wilmer was glad to be home. Usually, he preferred being in school, where he could learn and expand his scientific knowledge. But he couldn't bear to watch the throngs of kids talking about the wonderful Claudius—or Claudius's constant bragging about his incredible genius.

But the cure didn't work. Why couldn't everyone realize that? If only the other kids observed like Wilmer, then they would see the truth. Wilmer locked himself in his room and lay on his bed. He stared at the ceiling to think, but all he thought was that his ceiling was extremely boring.

He needed to observe more. That's how great science is born. And he had a guinea pig just downstairs, likely racing around the kitchen table right at that very second.

Wilmer needed to stop feeling sorry for himself and get to work. If the Claudius Cure didn't cure, then Wilmer was wasting his time fretting. The school still needed him, whether it knew it or not.

Surprisingly, Sherman was not running in circles. Instead he was watching cartoons, although he ran in place as he watched them, eating a glowing bowl of Marshmallow FruityBUZZZZ! cereal. Wilmer went to stand next to him with a magnifying glass and peered closely at Sherman's blinking rainbow skin. He poked him twice, gently. Sherman paid him no attention.

From the television the deep voice of Guy Dimples rang out, startling Wilmer, who stopped poking and looked up. "We interrupt this program for an urgent message."

On the screen Gwendolyn Bray stood in front of

Mumpley Middle School. Yesterday she had smiled and giggled with Claudius. But today she wore a stern, serious expression. She stared at the camera. She spoke with urgency. "This is Gwendolyn Bray. The Mumpley epidemic appears to be spreading unchecked. Previously this colorful contagion had been limited to students at Mumpley Middle School, but no longer. The third-to-fifth-grade elementary school has reported many severe cases, with half the class blinking like holiday lights. In fact, there are reports of random Christmas caroling from class to class. Schools across town are starting to report similar disturbances. In one local kindergarten a red, white, and blue boy so resembled an American flag that his entire class faced him while reciting the Pledge of Allegiance. As you might expect, this was extremely traumatic for the five-year-old, who was then forced to recite his pledge while looking in a mirror."

The screen shifted. It began showing taped news clips featuring students around town.

A second grader sneezed in front of her house. Red and black squares covered her head. "It's horrible! People keep asking to play checkers on me!" she sobbed. Wilmer stared closely. She held a carton of the Claudius Cure, just visible in the corner of the screen.

Next the scene on TV switched to the Frozen-BUZZZZ! ice-cream parlor downtown. A boy stood in front of the building. He was a particularly horrendous shade of bright red, with splotches of small black dots. His hair was green. He held an ice-cream cone, and Wilmer recognized the flavor as Watermelon Delight. It was the exact same color as the boy. "I don't know what's happening," he said between licks. "People keep calling me Watermelon Boy. I hate watermelon!"

"You're eating watermelon ice cream," the reporter said from off camera.

"Yeah, but this is ice cream, so it doesn't count."

Lastly, the television cut to a high school girl. Her crimson spots looked like an unfortunate case of acne. She buried her face in one hand and shouted, "I'm so embarrassed! Go away! Go away!" In her other hand was a ChocoChipBUZZZZ! brownie bar.

Sherman raced to the kitchen to run a few laps around the table. He completed his orbit in 3.72 seconds. Impressive.

On TV, Gwendolyn Bray was speaking with Milner Myerson. His minty green face matched the green MintyBUZZZZ! cookie he held. While he spoke, he also ran in circles.

Back in the kitchen Sherman swallowed his last few bites of Marshmallow FruityBUZZZZ! cereal and started his next table lap, this time a little faster.

On TV, Milner Myerson continued running.

Wilmer turned to watch Sherman's running.

He pivoted back to Milner running.

Back to Sherman running.

Suddenly a light turned on in Wilmer's head, and not a colorful fluorescent blinking light, but a plain white inspiring one. He leaped not once, but twice. Wilmer would recognize that hyperactive reaction anywhere. Sugar! Sugar gave you energy. Sugar made you want to zip and zing.

What if everyone was eating too much sugar?

But everyone was *always* eating sugar.

What if everyone was eating too much Sugar-BUZZZZ!?

Wilmer gasped as the idea lightbulb in his brain grew even brighter. What if the *contagion bacteria* loved SugarBUZZZZ!?

It all made sense! That might be why Wilmer hadn't caught the disease—or at least why he hadn't shown any symptoms. He avoided SugarBUZZZZ! Without any of that sugary stuff in his body, the bacteria didn't have anything to eat, so it couldn't grow. Meanwhile, Sherman was fluttering with color, and he practically lived on SugarBUZZZZ!-infested foods.

But a theory wasn't fact. Wilmer had to prove it scientifically. And after he proved it, he still needed to find a cure. *If* he could find a cure.

There was only one flaw to his plan. Claudius had caught the disease, but he was allergic to SugarBUZZZZ! So why had he shown such severe symptoms? Wilmer wondered if maybe there was more to Claudius's miraculous recovery than Claudius was letting on.

Wilmer glanced back at the television, where

Gwendolyn Bray was once again live, speaking in front of the school. "When will this horror end?" she said. "When heroes like our own Claudius Dill can't stop the spread of this disease, who can? This is Gwendolyn Bray. And that's nothing but the truth."

Sherman was about to drink a large glass of thick, sapphire-colored Blueberry MilkBUZZZZ! from the table. But this time Wilmer snatched it first, leaving Sherman shrieking in anger. "Sorry! Science calls!" said Wilmer, dashing upstairs to his lab. He raced inside his room, almost tripping on the pair of garden-dirt-crusted boots he had left by the door the day before, and locked the door behind him.

III.

Wilmer's hands trembled as he lowered an eye-dropper into the SugarBUZZZZ!-laced liquid. He then removed Ernie's glowing green tissue from last week. He carefully squeezed the dropper, and one blue-tinted MilkBUZZZZ! droplet dripped out. Wilmer was so quiet you could hear a pin drop, or more accurately, a MilkBUZZZZ! drop as it plopped onto the tissue.

The tissue glowed a brief but radiant bright lime. Excited, Wilmer dropped another drop onto the tissue.

The formula blinked and then glowed so brilliantly Wilmer had to cover his eyes. The green spread throughout the tissue all the way to its edges!

Wilmer bubbled with excitement, even more than the specimen on his desk was bubbling. Now he was onto something. This could be the breakthrough he had hoped for. He slid over the microscope he had borrowed from class. He put Ernie's tissue under the lens and peered through the eyepiece.

Amazing! Small and spiky bright blue molecules of blueberry-colored MilkBUZZZZ! swam alongside large, fuzzy, oddly shaped green-glowing ones. Those must be Ernie's nasal mucus germs. They were shaped sort of like Mr. Dooley—tall, thin, and slightly stooped. But wait. The tall green molecules were eating the blue ones! Every time a blue molecule bumped against a green one, the green molecule devoured it and rapidly ballooned.

Wilmer stared in astonishment.

After eating, these new compounds quickly flickered from blue to green to red and then purple. Some then appeared to burp. The entire formula fizzed and snapped. The process repeated itself over and over and over again, until the Mr. Dooley–shaped molecules had consumed every last spiky blue molecule.

It was the breakthrough Wilmer needed. This process must be repeating itself every time anyone ate or drank something with SugarBUZZZZ! Those odd Mr. Dooley–shaped germs were harmless inside each kid until they came into contact with SugarBUZZZZ! and then *bam!* Those green bacteria swallowed it as eagerly as Sherman did his Halloween candy.

But where did those fuzzy green germs come from in the first place?

And—Wilmer gulped three times in a row—what would happen if word about SugarBUZZZZ! leaked out?

Unless Wilmer found a cure, his father could be disgraced and his career ruined. No one would care about his new invention. SugarBUZZZZ! was feeding the plague! Who would trust anything from the man who turned Mumpley Middle School into a blinking rainbow of hyperactivity?

He had to be sure about his theory before he could make his next move. "Sherman!" cried Wilmer, opening his door. "Come quick!" Sherman bounded up the steps two at a time.

"I was busy running around the table," said Sherman.

"You can do that later. I need your help. Here! Drink this!" Wilmer handed him the giant glass of Blueberry MilkBUZZZZ!

"Hey, that's mine!" said Sherman, yanking the glass from Wilmer's hand and drinking its entire contents in one extended gulp.

The reaction was immediate. Sherman's ears flashed blue, blinking from baby blue to an electric blue to teal. But that was nothing compared with the surge of manic energy that hit Sherman like a runaway locomotive. He immediately spun in place twelve times, bounced on Wilmer's bed five times, and did a Russian bottle dance while balancing the now-empty glass of MilkBUZZZZ! on his head. His ears changed color with every dip of his knees.

It was so obvious! Wilmer could scarcely believe he hadn't noticed the connection before.

It was no wonder the contagion was getting stronger inside his sugar-addled classmates. They were stuffing themselves with more and more SugarBUZZZZ! treats every minute of the day. Every snack they ate, the bacteria ate too, growing bigger and bigger and making the infection worse and worse.

But there was still something that bothered Wilmer, one element that dangled like an enthusiastically pulled loose sweater thread: Claudius, and the Claudius Cure. How had Claudius been infected when he had a SugarBUZZZZ! allergy? He would never have had any of those spiky blue molecules in his system, so the bacteria would have had nothing to eat and thrive on. Claudius shouldn't have shown any colorful symptoms. But he had. Wilmer had seen it himself! Claudius was the one weak link in Wilmer's theory.

He needed to test a sample of the Claudius

Cure. What was in it? If he could prove it was phony, he'd prove Claudius was a fraud once and for all. Unfortunately, Claudius had announced that he was sold out until next week. Wilmer considered calling Ernie. His traitorous former best friend had held a carton yesterday. Maybe he had some cure left? But there was no way Wilmer was calling that rat. He wouldn't give Ernie the satisfaction!

So who else?

Roxie. She had been in line. Maybe she still had some cure left. The thought of asking her made his knees buckle and his jaw tighten. But this was too important for him to chicken out now. He just needed to practice talking to her.

Calm. Cool. How would Zane Bradley ask?

"Hey, Roxie baby. What's shaking? Like, have any cure?" Wilmer winced. That wouldn't work at all. He just wasn't the calm and cool type.

Strong. Silent. Wasn't that what girls liked?

"Cure. Now. Give me." No, that wouldn't work either. Wilmer sounded like a deranged caveman.

Suave. Debonair. Maybe with a British accent?

"'Ello, Roxie. Tip-top day, eh? D'ya have any cure? Chop-chop, lassie. Cheerio!" Eck. That was weird and creepy at the same time, although also strangely sophisticated.

Maybe he should just be natural.

"Hi, Roxie. I was wondering if you had any Claudius Cure left? I need some for a science experiment."

Ack! That was the worse option yet! He sounded . . . like himself. Well, he'd think of something. He leaped up and dashed from the room. The sooner he got that cure, the sooner he could get back to work.

"Where are you going?" asked Mrs. Dooley, stirring a giant pot of something that smelled like onions, asparagus, and foot fungus cream. Wilmer rushed out the door with only a wave, and without inhaling another whiff.

IV.

Wilmer had been in Roxie's house once before, during her grade-wide eleventh birthday party last year. He wore a tie and jacket, which turned out to be a mistake, since it was a swimming party (he had been so excited that he hadn't read the invitation carefully). He barely spoke to Roxie that day, and sat on a lounge chair sweating in his necktie while everyone else splashed and swam. But it was one of his most cherished memories, anyway. He could still picture nearly every moment of the party and every item in her house as if he were standing there that very moment. At the party his cupcake had part of a frosting R on it, for "Roxie." He could barely believe his luck! Instead of eating his birthday dessert, he carefully cupped the cupcake in his hand and carried it home after the party ended. Too bad Mom added it to her dinner pot the following week when she made her mustard-infused catfish quinoa wraps for dinner. If not, he might have kept it forever.

Wilmer had walked by Roxie's house 142 times since that party. He had considered knocking on her door 139 of those 142 times (98 percent!) but hadn't dared.

But this was in the name of science! Science wasn't for the meek. Wilmer took a deep breath and rang the doorbell. Someone was coming. Wilmer realized he still hadn't decided what he was going to say or how to say it, and he was completely flummoxed when Roxie answered the door.

"Yes?" she asked.

Wilmer blushed, swayed, and took a deep breath. "Hi, Roxie," he muttered. "You're looking very pink. Pinkish. I like pink, you know. I mean, it's not my favorite color or anything. Blue is my favorite color. But pink is right up there. After green, purple, and red." Wilmer bit his lip so he would shut up.

"Thanks, I think?" said Roxie.

"And after yellow and orange," continued Wilmer. "But it's before other colors."

"I don't think there are any other colors, actually."

"Oh. Well, it's nice. But not as nice as blue, at least in terms of my favorite colors." Why couldn't Wilmer just keep his mouth shut? Normally, he was tongue-tied around her, and now he couldn't keep his gums from flapping. "I like lots of shades of blue, but I lean toward a royal blue, or more of an azure, really."

"I like blue too," said Roxie, smiling. "And I like your color, I guess. What is it?"

"Um, plain?" suggested Wilmer.

"It fits you."

Wilmer smiled and felt his checks blush. "Pink suits you, too. I mean after green or purple or red or yellow or orange. But it's right up there after that." Maybe if Wilmer wished it very hard, he could go backward in time three minutes and start over. Time travel would be his next science experiment. "But any color would look good on you!" he blurted out.

Roxie smiled. "That's sweet. But why are you here, Wilmer?"

Wilmer's mind went blank. He stared at Roxie and suddenly couldn't remember who he was, why he was there, or even what language he spoke. Spanish? German? English? It was like someone had taken an eraser and rubbed out his entire mind. "Um, er, uh," said Wilmer.

"Okay, well, I'm glad you like the color blue," said Roxie, stepping back. "And other colors. I'll see you at school." She started to close the door.

"Wait!" shouted Wilmer a bit too loudly, startling Roxie. "Sorry. I remembered why I'm here. I saw you in line buying the Claudius Cure."

Roxie shrugged. "So did everyone."

"I know. But I was wondering if you had any left. Maybe? A little?"

Roxie smiled. "I started to drink it, but then I wondered why no one was actually being cured by the cure, you know? In school Claudius lost his zigzags almost immediately. So I started to think something was fishy. I know that's terrible of me to say."

"No!" said Wilmer. "It's not terrible. I was thinking the same thing. So I thought maybe I could test it and . . ."

"Because as a reporter, I'm supposed to question things," continued Roxie. "That's what reporters do. They observe and ask. Like Gwendolyn Bray on TV. And it just seemed like everyone was too trusting."

Wilmer nodded. "It's a scientist's job to observe too."

Roxie smiled. "I guess we're sort of alike,

then. You know, I never thought Claudius cured Copernicus, either. I always thought it was you."

Wilmer felt his head might be turning as pink as Roxie's. "Really?"

Roxie nodded. "Of course." She hesitated for a moment and then said, "Hold on." She ducked into the house and a moment later came out with a milk carton. "There's still most of it left in here. I don't want it."

"Can I have it? I need to see what it's made of. And see if Claudius was telling the truth."

Roxie handed the carton to Wilmer. For a moment their hands touched and Wilmer's heart fluttered. "If anyone can solve this mystery, it's you." She smiled, moved her hand away, and then went back inside the house.

Wilmer was too stunned to do anything other than stand there, melting into the porch. When he turned around and began heading home, he wasn't sure if he was walking or floating. He couldn't feel his feet or his head. They were soaring in the clouds somewhere high and distant, carried by an air current of hope.

V.

Wilmer made it back home, although he couldn't remember much about the walk. He floated upstairs to his room, still holding the milk carton. Her fingers had touched his hand! She thought he was smart! And he didn't even have to speak in an accent, either. She believed in him, and not in Claudius Dill.

But Wilmer needed to clear his head. For a scientist, being clearheaded is as important as keen observation skills. In fact, keen observation skills depend on clearheadedness. They go together like ice cream and cones! Peanut butter and jelly! Formaldehyde and dead biological specimens!

Behind his closed door Wilmer lifted the Ernie-snot-and-MilkBUZZZZ!-soaked tissue from earlier and slowly poured a few drops of Claudius Cure on it.

The tissue bubbled and shook. It jumped into the air by itself. And then the entire tissue burst into flames! Ashes of burning fibers tumbled through the air, twitching, a rain of glowing red confetti, like the sky after a fireworks explosion.

Wilmer hadn't expected that to happen.

Then Wilmer splashed the cure onto an empty glass slide and peered at it under the microscope. He instantly recognized the bouncing spiky molecules of SugarBUZZZZ! in all sorts of vibrant colors. That explained everything! This medicine *wasn't* medicine! It was just a bunch of different Sugar-BUZZZZ! flavors mixed together. If anything, just as Wilmer had suspected all along, the Claudius Cure made the contagion worse.

Wilmer grabbed his notebook and quickly jotted down his observations. His fingers trembled with excitement, which unfortunately made it impossible to read his writing. But no matter! He wouldn't soon forget these results.

Wilmer lay back on his bed, wanting to scream—in joy for uncovering Claudius's deceit, and in anger for his deceiving people at all. Instead the screams canceled each other out and he just sort of squeaked. He'd thought he would be happy to learn Claudius was a fake, but he wasn't. He was angrier than ever. When he thought of Claudius taking all that money from kids, and of his television appearance, Wilmer's brain turned into a raging storm cloud with lots of loud, crashing thunder. Science wasn't about glory; it was about facts. It was about truth! Claudius wasn't just a fake—he was against everything science stood for.

But Wilmer didn't have any more time to waste on Claudius—the town was depending on him. He sat on his bed and took deep breaths. He needed to be clearheaded, now more than ever.

He'd prove that Claudius Dill was nothing but a cheat. He'd prove that true, honest science made a difference. And most of all he'd prove to Roxie that her faith in him hadn't been a mistake.

FRIDAY
Day 11

Dear Journal,

By the time I arrived at school this morning, a line already snaked out from Claudius's locker. Apparently, he had squeezed out a small batch of Claudius Cure last night. Prices had doubled. For some reason kids still paid for it.

They refused to Observe—with a capital O!

The cure doesn't work. Can't everyone see that? The proof is right in front of their noses! For some kids the proof is actually blinking on their noses, from violet to yellow and back again.

I told eight different kids not to throw their money away, but they all ignored me. They're treating Claudius like a rock star. I saw Felix Frostmire buy Claudius's autograph from Caleb Koolidge for five dollars.

Interestingly, kids still glow and blink, but the colors seem duller than before. Sara Stapps's swirling scarlet spots are now more of an auburn, and Susie Pepperton's pulsating turquoise diamonds are closer to an asparagus.

My classmates also appear slightly less active, although it might be my imagination. But rather than climbing a tree upside down, Bern Whirley climbed it right side up. And the long chorus line of girl dancers looked slightly off step.

I passed Ernie in the school yard. His bright green head is now pistachio. He smiled and gave me a small wave as if he wasn't a traitorous backstabber. I turned my back to him and walked away. I wonder how much money he's wasted on Claudius Cure so far.

Why will no one listen to me when I say Claudius is a fraud? It's just like last semester, when people didn't believe me when I said Claudius didn't cure Copernicus the iguana. Maybe science isn't just about proving things. Maybe it's about convincing people of things too.

The astronomer and scientist Galileo lived four hundred years ago. Back then people believed the sun revolved around Earth. Galileo proved the opposite was true: Earth rotated around the sun. For his discovery he was thrown in jail.

I guess I'm not the only scientist with a major convincing problem. Hopefully, coming up with a cure won't get me thrown in jail. I just want to do some good.

Signing off,
Wilmer Dooley

I.

Wilmer ran up to everyone he saw that morning, yelling about his disturbing discovery: The Claudius Cure was phony! Claudius had merely mixed up some SugarBUZZZZ! It actually made the contagion worse, not better!

"It's fake!" he shouted to periwinkle-blinking Eric Eckersly.

"Don't drink that!" he warned the cool-blue-flickering Elvira Menkin.

But no one wanted to listen.

It might have helped if Ernie had been by his

side. Two people might convince a doubting public easier than one. Wilmer couldn't turn the tide washing over the school all by himself.

But Ernie and Wilmer weren't speaking. And Wilmer wasn't about to be the one to crack the ever-thickening walls of ice between them.

Susie Pepperton waved a large wad of cash. "I brought all my money today. I'm going to be cured!" she said to Wilmer. "Like you!"

"It doesn't work. Look around. People are more colored than a coloring book!" yelled Wilmer.

"You're not."

"I was never sick!"

"Cody Bimble said he's feeling a lot better."

Cody Bimble stood only a few feet away, covered in large, dull, purplish starbursts. He sneezed fourteen times in a row. "I feel great!" he said, and then sneezed six more times before breaking into a trembling coughing fit.

"See?" said Susie, walking away with her nose in the air.

In the hallway Roxie huddled with Vonda and Claire by their lockers. Roxie would back Wilmer up! She was on his side! And as Mumpley Middle School's star reporter, she was someone people would definitely believe.

When Wilmer thought back to their talk yesterday, he still felt tingly inside. It almost made him more wary of talking to her, as if their conversation had been a dream and speaking to her again would wake him from it. But she could help spread the word about Wilmer's discovery. He was sure of it. So he pushed aside his nerves and strode forward, holding his breath, chest out.

"What do you want?" said Vonda, sneering from her coral-colored lips. Wilmer's puffed out chest deflated like a punctured bicycle tire.

He looked straight at Roxie, her bright pink face now a dingy salmon. "I was right," he said. "It's fake. Claudius made the whole thing up. The Claudius Cure is just a bunch of SugarBUZZZZ! mixed together."

"It cured me," said Claire, sniffling and then sneezing.

"You're still purple," said Wilmer. "Sort of a plum, actually."

"You say that like it's a bad thing," responded Claire, fluffing her hair.

"You're just jealous of Claudius, since he's better at science than you," snapped Vonda. "Because he helped Copernicus last semester."

"No he didn't! That was me!" said Wilmer, but Vonda rolled her eyes and slowly marched away. Claire followed.

Roxie lingered for a second, until Vonda demanded, "Roxie? Are you coming?" Roxie looked over to Wilmer, glanced back at Vonda, and then turned and followed her friend, walking off with small, slow baby steps.

Wilmer stood in the hallway, stunned. Roxie acted as if they hadn't talked yesterday at all.

But he was even more struck by Roxie's walk. She seemed almost sluggish. There was no doubt she had less zip. Yes, he was certain of it. Some kids *did* have less pep in their step.

Drabber colors. Reduced energy. This could mean one of a couple of things. First, that the epidemic was ending on its own. Second, and much more likely, that it was reaching a different phase of infection, just as Wilmer had feared. If so, he needed to find a cure immediately—or it might mutate into so many different strains that it would be too late to *ever* stop the disease.

II.

Wilmer brooded at lunch. He sat by himself now. Ernie ate with Chuck Chen and Ronny Roswick at a different table. Roxie and her gang sat far away too. No one wanted to talk to a normal-tinted kid and listen to his seemingly bogus claims about the Claudius Cure. They didn't want to hear the truth. Especially not from Wilmer.

If only he were a blue whale. Blue whales emitted loud sounds that could be heard for hundreds of miles underwater, reaching up to 188 decibels. That was even louder than a jet plane. Then maybe people would listen!

But not only was he not a blue whale, he wasn't even blue! His epidermis was the same boring color as always.

He needed to find someone who could tell the entire school the truth; someone who could screech the facts loudly across the school where everyone could hear. Someone people would believe.

But there *was* a way. Of course! The PA system. Kids would believe Principal Shropshire.

Wilmer hated to tattle on Claudius for making a false cure, but he couldn't just sit around and do nothing. Principal Shropshire was a little befuddled sometimes, but he would listen to reason. He had to! Wilmer scooped up his last spoonful of creamed spinach, gulped it down, and marched straight out of the lunchroom.

He hurried down the hall and to the main office, confident the principal could be convinced to help spread the word. Wilmer had never been inside the principal's office before. He wasn't the sort of kid who got in trouble, and only kids who got in trouble went to the principal's office.

"I need to see Principal Shropshire!" Wilmer announced to Mrs. O'Brien, the principal's secretary.

She yawned. "What did you do?"

"Nothing."

Mrs. O'Brien narrowed her eyes. "You want to see the principal, but you aren't in trouble?"

Wilmer nodded.

"I've never heard of such a thing," she muttered. "I suppose you can go in. But he's very busy. It better be important."

Wilmer assured her that it was.

The principal sat behind voluminous stacks of paper arranged haphazardly around his desk. His thick, black-rimmed black glasses sat at the edge of his nose as he examined some pages filled with numbers. His right arm hung out of view, under the desk. He looked up. "Oh, hello. What have you done wrong? No matter. Just don't do it again. Good day." He resumed looking at his papers. "I'm very busy."

"I haven't done anything wrong," said Wilmer. "I need to talk."

Principal Shropshire looked up and his eyes narrowed. "You've come to see me, but you aren't in trouble? I've never heard of such a thing. Well, I'm afraid I don't have time to talk. I mean, I'm talking now, I realize, so it's not like my time doesn't allow me the ability to talk, I hope that's quite clear. No, I'm busy with this colorful calamity that has created quite a conundrum. Ha! That's a tongue twister, like 'Seashells she shells,' or rather, 'She shells seashells.' No, that's not it. Well, no matter. But I have lots to do. News reporters want to talk. Doctors are puzzled. Parents are on edge. If it weren't for students like Claudius Dill, who knows what would become of us?" Principal Shropshire thumbed through a stack of papers on his desk. "We have fire drills and tornado drills, but nothing about color drills. Did you know that if you search for *colorful drill* on the Internet, you get a list of oddly hued dental instruments?"

"Well, that's what I want to talk about," interjected Wilmer.

"You want to become a dentist?" asked Principal Shropshire. "A fine choice. We can never have enough dentists, I always say. Just last week I was telling Mrs. O'Brien the world needs more orthodontists. Or was it orthopedic shoes? I get those confused all the time. Well, no matter. I'm busy. It was a pleasure talking." He shuffled some more papers, carefully stacking them higher and higher.

"I don't want to be a dentist. Although it is a noble profession," Wilmer added.

"It is," said Principal Shropshire, nodding and picking at his teeth.

But Wilmer was growing impatient with Principal Shropshire's blabbering. "I need to talk about the Claudius Cure. I think it's doing more harm than good. No one is getting better. They're getting worse."

Principal Shropshire paused his paper shuffling. "I admit I haven't seen much progress. I've seen progress in the world, like the invention of the flat-screen television, but I'm referring to progress with the Claudius Cure, of course. These things take time. Besides, people say they're feeling better." Principal Shropshire raised his hand—which had been hidden under his desk—to scratch his forehead. It was teal with lavender spots.

"Your hand!" said Wilmer, despite himself.

The principal blushed and quickly ducked his hand back under the desk. "Oh! That. Yes. No matter. Our little secret, no? But as you can see, I have plenty of things to do. Now run along."

"But the Claudius Cure!" said Wilmer.

"Yes, good for him!" said the principal. "Busy,

busy, busy." Wilmer noticed three empty milk cartons in the trash can next to Principal Shropshire's desk, a few drops of green liquid crusted on their side. A speck of green flashed on the principal's lips. "I only wish the cure weren't so expensive," he mused.

As Wilmer turned, frustrated, he nearly plowed into Mrs. Padgett, who was walking into the office. "Excuse me. Sorry," he huffed, rushing out.

III.

Mrs. Padgett closed the door behind her. "I've come to talk about Wilmer Dooley," she spat.

"Who? Oh, the boy who was just here. Fine boy. Yes. But if you'll excuse me, I'm a bit too occupied for chitchat." The principal gestured to the papers around him.

Mrs. Padgett sat down. Principal Shropshire was too busy for the chair of the school Science Department, co-chair of the school Detention Program, and co-co-chair of the school Chair Cleaning Committee? Nonsense! "That boy is up to no good. I've seen him working in my lab, using my supplies.

Now a microscope is missing. We're talking Grade A thievery, Principal Shropshire. Unforgivable mischief!" She pounded her fist on the desk, and a towering stack of papers teetered over. Principal Shropshire frowned.

"No need for dramatics," he said. "Not that I don't like the theater every now and again. I'm fond of musicals, myself. I quite enjoyed watching the students perform *Annie* last year."

Mrs. Padgett pounded the desk again. Three more paper stacks fell. Principal Shropshire winced. "May I remind you that fourteen test tubes are missing too?" she said. "What's next? The desks? The chairs? The new vibrating massage table in the teacher's lounge? Something must be done!" She pounded the desk yet again. The remaining seven paper piles collapsed. Principal Shropshire groaned.

"Really, Mrs. Padgett," he said, after staring at the helpless heap of papers now covering his desk. "I'm quite busy with this contagion crisis and paper stacking. We must be steadfast! Focused! Now, what do you think of this Claudius Cure going around?

Does it work? I've heard rumors that it might not yield results quite as advertised." He glanced at the trash can next to his desk with the cartons sitting in it.

"I can personally vouch for Claudius Dill," Mrs. Padgett said briskly. "He cleans my whiteboards, you know. I can assure you his character is unimpeachable."

"Really, Mrs. Padgett, peaches have nothing to do with the matter."

"I said *unim*peachable. He is quite trustworthy, I assure you."

"That reminds me, I need to eat lunch. If only peaches were in season. I'm quite a fan of them. I also like dentists. The world needs more peaches and dentists, I always say. And musicals. Now run along. And if you learn anything new about this crisis, please come in. We need a breakthrough, not more nonsense. If only someone could discover what is causing it! Well, someone must, anyway. Eventually."

"But—"

"Good day."

IV.

Back at his house Wilmer sat on the couch, ignoring Sherman's headstands. He suggested that Sherman might want to put down the CrunchBUZZZZ! snack he was chewing until he was right-side up, but Sherman wouldn't hear of it. Wilmer couldn't even persuade his own brother to avoid these hazardous sweets. How would he be expected to convince the world?

But just like the students at school, Sherman also appeared to be slowing down. He performed only four headstands, then he raced into the kitchen and around the table in 4.6 seconds, nearly 24 percent slower than the other day.

Wilmer was deep in thought when Sherman jogged—jogged, not ran!—back into the room and turned on the television. More cartoons, no doubt. Wilmer had never particularly enjoyed cartoons; he preferred watching amoebas floating in a solution upstairs in his lab. But he immediately perked up when, instead of inane 'toon chatter, he heard the voice of Gwendolyn Bray in the middle of yet another late-breaking news flash.

Gwendolyn Bray held a carton of Claudius Cure and wore a very determined look on her face. "So please stop using any Claudius Cure. It is not effective against the disease, and there is strong evidence to suggest it might actually make the symptoms worse. I repeat, any Claudius Cure remaining should be discarded immediately."

Wilmer couldn't believe what he heard. Had people finally come to their senses? If so, how? Why?

He bounded upstairs to his room, switched his door sign from WELCOME to DO NOT DISTURB, SCIENCE IN PROGRESS, and then stepped inside, stumbling over the pair of dirty boots he still hadn't put away.

Grumbling, he lifted the boots to move them to the other side of the room, and then stopped. His eyes fixated on the dirt crusted on the bottom of the sole. Dirt from his mother's garden. Dirt that softly glowed blue. A distinctly nondirtlike blue.

Wilmer grabbed a plastic bag and rubber gloves. He dashed back down the stairs. He nearly collided with Sherman, who was now walking around the kitchen table as if out for a late-night stroll. Wilmer hurried past him and out the door to his mother's garden.

He saw the footprints from his mad stomp the other night. Vegetables were trampled and stems were snapped. Wilmer felt a twinge of guilt, but he couldn't let that interfere with his investigation. Science had no room for guilt. He peered at the large patch of turnips mangled below him. They all glowed—some blue, some yellow, some pink. One turnip was a vibrant green and red plaid. Another turnip was polka-dotted on the top and striped on the bottom. Wilmer lifted that turnip from the ground and put it safely inside his plastic sample bag. He headed back upstairs, eager to inspect it more carefully.

Upstairs, under his school-borrowed microscope, Wilmer confirmed his hunch. The turnip teemed with the Mr. Dooley–shaped germ molecules, bubbling and bouncing wildly. There was only one explanation. Mrs. Dooley's garden must be the source of the epidemic!

"Dinner's ready!" Mrs. Dooley screamed from downstairs, interrupting Wilmer's examination.

He followed her shriek into the kitchen, a million thoughts racing inside his head.

Mr. Dooley was already at the table. He wore giant blue goggles that jutted out about ten inches from his face. Sherman jittered in his seat as usual, but less so than before. For example, he bounced his legs two times a second instead of the previous four times. But Sherman's now-rust-hued stripes flashed off and on as quickly as ever.

"Don't wear your goggles at the dinner table, dear," said Mrs. Dooley as she carted over a plate of oyster puree–maple syrup ham loaf, a particularly unappetizing pink and brown hunk of ground meat. Even Sherman seemed a bit disturbed by it, at least for a moment, before happily—but slowly—plunging a forkful into his mouth.

"How are your Sixth-Grade Science Medal entry efforts going, Wilmer?" asked Mr. Dooley, forgetting to remove his goggles.

"Encouraging," said Wilmer. "I think I've traced the color epidemic to its source. But I'm not sure how it spread to the kids at school."

"What color epidemic?" said Mrs. Dooley.

Then to Sherman she said, "It's not polite to strobe at the dinner table, dear." She turned back to Wilmer. "You were saying?"

"Never mind," said Wilmer, shaking his head.

"Let me know if you need my help," said Mr. Dooley. "I know a thing or two about science!"

"I'm going to do this by myself, Dad. But thanks."

"No shame in receiving assistance. Some of the greatest scientists had help. Did Ben Franklin hold the kite when he discovered electricity? Did Albert Einstein come up with his theory of relativity all by himself?"

"Yes and yes?"

"Well! Then those are bad examples. But still, just ask if you need assistance. Anytime! Unless I'm in the bathroom. Or working downstairs. Or sleeping. But other than that, anytime. Mostly."

"I'm fine, Dad." Wilmer could just glimpse the edge of his father's trophy-crammed shelf in the living room. He would earn his own trophies, his own way.

"Okay, son. But remember, Grandpa helped me

win the Sixth-Grade Science Medal with my slug-inspired entry."

Wilmer ate his ham loaf, not because it tasted good—it actually tasted horrendous—but because even scientists need to eat. But when his mom brought over her sarsaparilla cake for dessert, he passed on it. That didn't stop Sherman from asking for a third slice before he finished his first one.

But as the scent of sarsaparilla filled the room, Wilmer's brain began to churn. He leaped up. He had a thought. No, more than a thought. An inspiration!

Not too long ago his mom had made dinner using that distinctive, root-beer-smelling herb. He still cringed to think of those sarsaparilla scallop strips they ate.

Or of the sarsaparilla turnip muffins she put in his lunch box the next morning.

Mrs. Dooley should have known better than to give Wilmer muffins of any sort, since he never touched her sugary concoctions. Wilmer didn't like turnips, either. So when he had found himself sitting at the same table as Roxie and her friends (the first of two straight days of lunchtime bliss!), he had offered her the muffin. Wilmer knew that giving generous gifts, like chocolates and flowers, was the surest way to win a girl's heart. He had written that observation down in his new journal that very day! Wilmer wasn't sure if sarsaparilla turnip muffins counted as generous gifts, but it had been worth a shot.

Wilmer had handed Roxie the muffin. Roxie had put down her Strawberry SugarBUZZZZ! soft drink, took a few nibbles, grimaced, and passed it to Claire. Claire had shared some muffin with Ernie, who passed it to Vonda. Vonda hadn't cared for it, so she carried it over to Zane Bradley at a different table. Apparently, the idea of a sarsaparilla turnip muffin was so odd that lots of kids wanted to sample a taste. If the turnip bacteria had devoured the SugarBUZZZZ! inside each kid's body as quickly as it had under the microscope . . .

It would have reached epidemic-like proportions before lunch was even over! Coughing and wheezing had spread the plague ever since, with the kids who ate the most SugarBUZZZZ! foods showing the strongest symptoms.

Wilmer had solved the mystery! He let out a scream of joy.

"Yes?" asked Mrs. Dooley. "You screamed?"

"Nothing," said Wilmer. "Just excited."

"The smell of sarsaparilla will do that to you," said Mrs. Dooley, nodding. And then she let out her own yelp of joy, as did Mr. Dooley, Preston, and Sherman immediately after.

Wilmer went upstairs to lie down. His ears hurt from so much screaming, and his head hurt from so much scientific thinking. But he still had so much to discover.

After all, he now knew that the turnips had likely caused the epidemic. But this fact alone didn't get him any closer to a cure. The root vegetable might have been the very root of the problem—but how did the bacteria creep inside the turnips in the first place?

That was the last missing piece of this confounding contagious jigsaw puzzle.

SATURDAY
Day 12

Dear Journal,

I spent the morning working on my history paper about medieval diseases. I'm way behind on my schoolwork. I've had bigger, more colorful things to think about.

From my disease research I've learned some additional interesting facts about epidemics, and especially the bubonic plague. I'm not sure if they'll help me solve the Mumpley malady, but they can't hurt. Knowing the past makes us smarter about the present.

In the fourteenth century, things were significantly more disgusting than they are today. There was no toothpaste, so people cleaned their teeth with twigs. Since there was no running water, some people bathed only once a year, and they hardly ever washed their clothes. Rats ran around the streets. Without indoor plumbing, the toilet was just a hole in the floor. It was hardly ever cleaned. When it was, the stuff in the hole was just dumped in the middle of the street. Ugh! Filth and horrible smells were everywhere. Germs love filth. So diseases bubbled up and spread.

But you need more than germs to create an epidemic. You need people! The population kept growing and growing. Epidemics spread quickly when you get a lot of people crammed together, like in big cities. Or in a school lunchroom. A lunchroom is practically the perfect place for an epidemic to take hold.

Also, those so-called cures often made things worse. Doctors performed surgery using dirty equipment. They might stick red-hot pokers in you or mix odd herbs and spread them over your body. One cure for a cold was to cram mustard and onion up your nose.

But people wanted to believe doctors knew what they were doing, so patients did what they were told. Just like my starstruck schoolmates are convinced the Claudius Cure cures, even though it obviously doesn't. People will believe almost anything if they want to believe it enough.

If only doctors, patients, and the students at Mumpley Middle School would observe! Then they would see the truth! That's why science is so important. That's why observation is the most important tool we have.

I know I'll find a cure for this disease if I keep observing. I can do it.

I have to.

Signing off,
Wilmer Dooley

I.

Wilmer hoped he might stumble upon a cure through trial and error. His trial-and-error attempts hadn't gone very well when he attempted to win Roxie's affections. Still, he had to try. Sometimes solving a problem meant getting lucky. It meant observing at just the right time.

Wilmer coaxed Sherman into his room with the promise of new desserts. The now-olive-and copper-tinted Sherman crept up the stairs. He didn't jump or leap, but lumbered slowly. Wilmer actually had to help him up the final step! What was happening to him?

Up in his room Wilmer had laid out a series of test samples. He hoped Sherman wouldn't notice the desserts weren't really desserts at all, but rather odd food combinations that might counteract the effects of the bacteria.

"This looks like a cracker," said Sherman, hoisting the saltine and studying it.

The opposite of sweetness was saltiness, sort of. Wilmer wondered if the disease-carrying germs might be slowed with excess salt. Or if maybe the bacteria would lose their appetite. Wilmer had spread some mayonnaise on the cracker so that it looked dessert-like. "That's white chocolate. Really," said Wilmer. He hated to lie, but it was in the name of science.

Sherman sniffed it suspiciously. Luckily for Wilmer, Sherman's nose was completely stuffed. Despite the strange new side effects, the plague's cold-like symptoms seemed as strong as ever. Sherman took a bite, shrugged, and swallowed.

His spots flickered brightly once and then resumed their dreary tint.

Wilmer scribbled into his notebook: "Excessive amounts of salt: no change."

Next Wilmer handed Sherman a plate of peas. Maybe healthy vegetables would prove a formidable foe for this malady.

Sherman looked at the plate in disgust. "That's not dessert." He stuck his tongue out.

Wilmer had prepared for just such objections. "No. Those are boogers from my nose."

"Really?" said Sherman, peering closer at them. He pushed a pea to see what might happen. It rolled. "Boogers don't roll."

"These do. They're magic boogers."

"What sort of magic do they do?" asked Sherman suspiciously.

"It's a surprise."

Sherman tilted the plate so that the peas rolled into his mouth. "Not bad," he said. "But I don't feel magical."

"Exactly!" said Wilmer. "Um, they magically

stop magic from happening." Wilmer knew that made no sense, but Sherman nodded knowingly.

Again, though, nothing changed with Sherman's hue. Wilmer scribbled this observation into his notebook too.

Wilmer had eight more cures lined up. He gave each to Sherman, one at a time.

Sherman ate part of a sponge. Wilmer hoped it might soak up the SugarBUZZZZ! but it didn't.

Sherman ate a plateful of turnips from the grocery store. Wilmer wondered if regular turnips might counterbalance infected turnips.

Nope.

Sherman drank a vial of red food coloring. Wilmer wondered if his brother's multicolored body might stabilize and turn red, which wouldn't be a cure exactly, but it would be a step forward. For example, if Sherman turned bright red, then Wilmer could add yellow and make his brother orange and eventually find a color combination that matched Sherman's precontagion skin tone.

But the food coloring didn't do anything.

Next Wilmer thought of creamed spinach. Since Wilmer ate so much spinach, and he was healthy, maybe spinach was a natural antidote. He added a pinch of sugar. He knew Sherman would never eat spinach otherwise. But it didn't matter. Nothing happened.

Wilmer was missing something crucial. But what was it?

Because it was Saturday, Wilmer had plenty of time to reflect after Sherman had left. But sitting in his bedroom wasn't inspiring him. He thought of his father, in the middle of his own mysterious experiments in the basement. Wilmer considered asking Mr. Dooley for help. Twice he walked to the basement door to ask, both times intending to knock on it. But both times he stepped away, deterred by his father's strict NO ONE ALLOWED EXCEPT ME policy.

Back in his room Wilmer punched his pillow in frustration. He almost felt like surrendering. But no! It was *his* job to solve the problem. He would be like Benjamin Franklin, holding that kite alone in a lightning storm, braving obstacles in the name of science. Franklin had remained in that downpour clutching that kite even though he had recently lost his umbrella.

Wilmer would earn his scientist stripes, his own way, even if obstacles poured down on him and soaked him from head to toe.

He punched his pillow again. Why did solving problems have to be so hard?

II.

Valveeta Padgett did *not* like thinking about school on her weekends. Off days were her private time. She had a strict routine of yoga, online mah-jongg, gardening, and scientific textbook reading. She knew it might not be the most exciting life (although her online mah-jongg games could get quite riveting), but it was hers. She prided herself on the smoothness of her routine.

Yet today her routine was ruined, and it was all Wilmer Dooley's fault.

Her online mah-jongg game had been a disaster. Her team lost every game, and she made several careless mistakes, quite uncharacteristic of her normal shrewd play. Playing wrong tiles! Discarding both one cracks!

Even her textbook reading was in disarray. She read the same page in her scientific textbook twenty-six times, because each time she began to read, her thoughts wandered off and she lost track of where she was. Again. And again. Twenty-six times.

But she couldn't help it. That Wilmer Dooley had settled into her head and wouldn't meander off. She kept thinking of him lurking in her science lab. She imagined him at home, dancing a jig with her stolen microscope and test tubes. He should be thrown in jail! The key tossed away!

Principal Shropshire was too soft. That was the problem. Kids needed to be punished for their crimes, not ignored. If she were principal, Wilmer Dooley would be expelled, and hung by his trousers from a flagpole. Well, maybe not the flagpole part. As much as she would enjoy that, she knew some parents might object to the flag not being raised to its proper position.

She was also crestfallen to discover that

Claudius had been discredited. Just the other day she had talked with Mr. Polansky, the chemistry teacher and her cojudge of the Sixth-Grade Science Medal. He had agreed that if the Claudius Cure worked at all, Claudius would easily earn the prestigious sixth-grade prize. But now? No one could claim it worked as advertised, not even her.

She didn't think she could give Claudius the award just for cleaning her whiteboards. A shame, really. But if Claudius didn't win, who would?

Not Wilmer Dooley. That's all she really cared about. It's not like he was running around creating cures, anyway. She recalled overhearing him tell students the Claudius Cure was a fake. It wouldn't have surprised her in the least if he had been the one to leak that information to the news media. She wouldn't put anything past him.

Her computer screen blinked. It was her turn for online mah-jongg. Distracted, she played a flower instead of the one bam. What was she thinking? Curse the luck!

It was all Wilmer Dooley's fault too. He was the misplayed mah-jongg tile of her life! She scratched a mosquito bite. No doubt that was his fault as well.

Everything was his fault.

III.

Claudius Dill sat in his room, staring at the empty milk jug on his desk. He had planned to spend the night mixing more Claudius Cure. But then the news had broken that it didn't work. He was out of business, just like that.

It was all Wilmer Dooley's fault, he was sure of it. Who else would have tipped off Gwendolyn Bray?

Claudius had converted part of his room into a science lab, with a large, professional-caliber microscope, test tubes of all sizes, various weights and measures, flasks and beakers, tongs, and even a high-quality desiccator for preserving moisture-sensitive items. All purchased for Claudius by his father, the World's Greatest Doctor. Claudius had never used half the equipment. He didn't even know why he needed a desiccator. But it was on a list of "Science Lab Equipment Basics" Claudius once found on a website, and it looked scientific.

He was sure Wilmer Dooley didn't have anything as impressive as this.

Claudius might have been disgraced by this Claudius Cure debacle. But he wouldn't just give up. No, he would get his revenge.

He looked down at the EVIL GENIUS T-shirt he wore. Wilmer Dooley would be sorry he had messed with Claudius Dill.

Very sorry.

From out in the hallway Claudius heard the distinctive and powerful footsteps of his father, the esteemed Dr. Fernando Dill, MD, PhD, AOCN, AARCF, BVMS, CHES, CLPNI, CST, DCP, DPH, DSM, and about 126 other degrees that went far down the alphabet. His clatter, loud and filled with determination and verve, was immediately identifiable.

"Dad!" said Claudius, hurrying into the hallway.

His father strode with long, determined steps. He wore a tuxedo. He stopped and looked down, surprised. "Hmmm? Oh, is that you, Clarius?"

"It's Claudius, Dad."

"Yes, Clavius."

"Claudius. With a *d*. Are you still trying to

discover a cure for this mysterious Mumpley plague?" If Dr. Dill solved the problem, Claudius could still be a hero. He could help! Father and son! The dynamic duo! The contagion couple!

"Not yet. No time. I'm off to Nova Scotia for a major medical conference. And then golf. I'm only home for a moment."

"I can help," said Claudius eagerly.

"Oh?" said Dr. Dill. "Do you golf?"

"I mean with the cure. I can help you find one."

"You?" said Dr. Dill. He giggled. "Oh, that's rich! What do you know about science?"

Claudius frowned. "I have a lab in my bedroom."

Dr. Dill blinked. "Really? Since when?"

"Since you bought it for me. So I can, you know, assist you with doing stuff."

"Clarius, please!" said Dr. Dill. "I have more than one hundred twenty-six medical abbreviations. Do you know how long it takes to sign my name? Eight hundred twenty-four seconds! I've counted. How many abbreviations do you have?"

"None," admitted Claudius, hanging his head.

"Exactly right. Now please. I'm in a bit of a hurry. I'll be back in a week or so."

"Then can we catch a ball game?" yelled Claudius as his father charged off. "You promised we could go."

"Yes! Soon! I'm sure I can squeeze in some time away next year. Or maybe the year after that. Before you start high school. Or college. How old are you again? Maybe you can go with your mother."

Claudius stood alone in the hallway as the World's Greatest Doctor trotted down the stairs. If only Claudius had some initials after his name. Then things would be different.

He'd just have to show his father what he was made of in other ways.

Like by taking down Wilmer Dooley.

SUNDAY
Day 13

Dear Journal,

Every great scientist has had a stumbling block or four. Sometimes observation isn't enough. Sometimes you need inspiration.

Sir Isaac Newton discovered gravity when an apple fell on the ground next to him. He wondered why an apple fell straight down toward the earth, rather than sideways or up. That inspiration formed the basis for his theory of gravitation. He used gravity to explain lots of things, including the orbit of the moon and planets.

Inspiration! Observation!

I observed that the closer you stand to the middle of the dodgeball court, the more it hurts when a ball is hurled at your nose. So now I stand in the back.

Inspiration! Observation! The two cruxes of scientific formulas and fact.

But sometimes maybe observation needs a hand. Maybe it's okay to get a little help, like Dad says. Most of the greatest scientists probably did have help making their discoveries. They worked in labs with assistants. They shared theories with colleagues. Ben Franklin had someone hold his kite while he went to the bathroom.

Sir Isaac Newton himself once said, "If I have seen further, it is by standing on the shoulders of giants." Maybe it's time I solicited help. After all, the greatest science giant I know is in my basement right now.

Dad said he won the Sixth-Grade Science Medal with a little assistance from Grandpa. Asking Dad to help me doesn't mean I'm a failure. It just means that I'm a scientist.

Signing off,
Wilmer Dooley

I.

Wilmer stood at the doorway into the basement. In front of him hung the large sign that had been posted for as long as Wilmer could remember:

NO ONE ALLOWED EXCEPT ME.
NO EXCEPTIONS.
ESPECIALLY NOT FOR YOU.

And then, in much smaller type:

ALSO, NO KNOCKING, EITHER,

UNLESS THE HOUSE IS ON FIRE.

AND THEN THE HOUSE BETTER BE VERY, VERY ON FIRE.

—IGNATIUS P. DOOLEY

Although the sign told him quite plainly not to knock, and even though Wilmer knew that right at this very moment his father was working on his mysterious experiments, and despite the small explosion he'd just heard from the basement, followed by a shout and the sound of glass breaking, Wilmer knocked.

He stood and waited. He heard another explosion, another shout, and more shattering glass.

He knocked again.

Finally he heard footsteps coming up the stairs. Wilmer held his breath as the door opened.

Mr. Dooley wore giant fuzzy brown aviator goggles. His charred hair curled up like a clown wig. Soot covered his face and his lab coat.

"Dad, are you okay?" asked Wilmer, alarmed.

"Of course," said Mr. Dooley. "Is the house very, very on fire?" he asked. He looked to the right and left frantically. "I don't see smoke."

"No, Dad. The house isn't on fire. I just had to talk."

Mr. Dooley frowned and wiped a smudge of soot from his ear. "Did you read the sign?" he asked, pointing to the door.

"Yes, Dad. I know it's against the rules. But I need help."

Mr. Dooley frowned. "I was in the middle of an important experiment! Very important! One so important that even if the house were very, very on fire, I might have been compelled to stay downstairs until the house turned very, very, very on fire."

"But I need another scientist's opinion. And you're the greatest scientist I know."

His dad unstooped his back, just slightly. "Well, I suppose just this once," he said, tilting his chin up. "Scientist to scientist, and all."

Mr. Dooley carefully closed the basement door and walked Wilmer over to the family room. They avoided Sherman, who was shuffling in circles around the kitchen table. Wilmer silently timed his lap: *One one thousand, two one thousand.* He estimated that Sherman circled the table in 8.6 seconds.

Father and son walked to the recliner and ottoman, where they took their usual seats.

"Did I tell you about that time fireflies inspired SugarBUZZZZ!?" Mr. Dooley asked. "I was allergic to flowers—"

"I know, Dad. I'm sorry. It's a great story. But I need to talk about the epidemic that's going around school."

"An epidemic around school?" asked Mr. Dooley, shocked. "What sort of epidemic?"

"People are changing colors. Like Sherman."

"Sherman is changing colors?" said Mr. Dooley. "I hadn't noticed."

"He's sea green with puce-tinged polka dots."

"I assumed it was just a phase," said Mr. Dooley. "Like when you took up skydiving."

"I've never tried skydiving."

"Oh. Never mind, then." Mr. Dooley shrugged. "You had something to tell me?"

Wilmer nodded. Then he took a deep breath. He hadn't spoken of the night he trampled his mother's garden. He was afraid he might be punished. But he realized he needed to come clean if he was going to ask his father for help. "People are turning unnatural colors all over Mumpley. And I was mad that I couldn't solve the problem, so the other day I trampled Mom's garden. I know I should have admitted it sooner. I'm sorry."

Mr. Dooley furrowed his brow. "Go on."

"Afterward I noticed the bottoms of my boots were glowing fluorescent blue," said Wilmer, getting more excited as he spoke. "So I went outside and tested Mom's soil. Her turnips, actually. They had the same molecules in them as the samples I took from my sick classmates. I think the disease came from the turnips!"

"I see," said Mr. Dooley, lost in thought. "Very interesting findings."

"You're not mad I trampled Mom's garden?"

"It was in the name of science, right?" asked Mr. Dooley.

"Technically, it was in the name of a temper tantrum," said Wilmer.

"Well, close enough. To invent the telephone, Alexander Graham Bell broke all his mother's clothes hangers. Do you think she minded? Probably. But no matter. Besides, I hate turnips. Now, are there any other symptoms?"

"Some mild cold symptoms. And everyone seems to have all sorts of energy. Or at least had— they're all slowing down. You may have noticed Sherman lumbering around the kitchen table."

Mr. Dooley glanced over to the kitchen. "Why, look, he is! Is circling tables one of the symptoms? Are people walking around random household objects everywhere?"

"No. Just Sherman. He's been doing that for years. The point is that he was doing it abnormally fast, and now he's doing it abnormally slowly."

"Interesting." Mr. Dooley paused. When he spoke, he spoke quietly, speaking to himself as much as to Wilmer. "These symptoms are nearly exactly like those from the rejected batch of my new invention. I was doing tests on broccoli, you see, trying to perfect my new stroke of brilliance. But I couldn't get the formula right. The vegetables I tested were too unsteady. Instead of turning neon green or fluorescent magenta, they started flashing all sorts of colors and stripes and patterns. Even worse, they wouldn't sit still. Broccoli florets bounced around my lab like angry ferrets, zipping and zinging haphazardly. One almost hit me in the eye! Luckily, I was wearing goggles. Well, you can't serve vegetables that can poke you in the eye. Who would want to eat such a dangerous food item? So I had to reject the entire batch. A shame, too."

Wilmer sat at the edge of the ottoman. "That might be exactly it."

Mr. Dooley continued talking softly, as if recalling horrible memories. "Of course, that wasn't the worst part." He shivered.

"What *was* the worst part?" asked Wilmer.

"The vegetables remained bouncy and twittery for a number of days. I had to put them in jars to keep them from flailing about the room. But they slowed and slowed. Their colors became drabber too. Then finally . . . well, it's not important," he said suddenly. "Nothing to worry about."

"Tell me," said Wilmer, getting anxious.

"Well, not to sound alarming, but they all exploded. *Bam!* A million pieces. The jars shattered too. What a mess. But as I said, I was wearing goggles. So no worries!"

Wilmer gulped. His gaze darted to the kitchen, where Sherman continued to trudge slower and slower. *One one thousand, two one thousand . . .* 10.4 seconds to circle the table.

His sixth-grade classmates had been moving slower in school the other day too. Especially Roxie.

Roxie!

An image of Roxie blowing into a million pieces smacked Wilmer in the head like an errant Frisbee. He jumped up. This was no longer about him winning a science medal or colors clashing with kids' clothing. It wasn't even about him winning the heart of his one true love.

His entire class was in jeopardy of exploding. He needed to save them. All of them. Now!

"I think it's time!" announced Mr. Dooley.

"Time to help me find a cure? Time to warn all the kids that they could explode at any moment?" said Wilmer, nodding eagerly.

"What? No. This is more important. A scientist never reveals what he's working on until he's ready. I suppose I'm ready. Call the family! Bring them downstairs! I'm going to show you all my brand-new invention!"

II.

Wilmer followed his father to the basement. Mrs. Dooley trailed next, carrying Preston. Sherman was last, plodding in an almost turtlelike crawl, his shoulders sagging.

Wilmer had been in his father's lab only once, two years ago, to bring him the kitchen fire extinguisher. He had thought about the basement lab equipment often, but it was even more impressive than he remembered. The financial success of SugarBUZZZZ! had allowed his father to upgrade the lab considerably. There was a state-of-the-art dual ion beam and scanning electron microscope, able to detect elements down to a single atom. There were large, complicated calibrated weights and scales. Lasers. Spectroscopes. And even more things Wilmer didn't recognize and could only begin to fathom what they might do. The only thing missing was a kitchen sink.

Mr. Dooley stood in front of a large table covered by a black cloth. The family sat on the floor.

"I need to get back to dinner," said Mrs. Dooley. "We're having Hawaiian-Ecuadorian Surprise."

"What's that?" asked Wilmer.

Mrs. Dooley shrugged. "How do I know? It's a surprise."

"Celery seed!" said Preston.

"Excellent suggestion," cooed Mrs. Dooley, rubbing Preston's head.

"Hush!" said Mr. Dooley. "I'm about to disclose my remarkable invention—a new creation that will change the way kids eat forever! When I invented SugarBUZZZZ! I was inspired by a firefly. There I was in the garden, sneezing—"

"Get on with it, dear," said Mrs. Dooley. Wilmer sighed in relief.

"Well, kids love fireflies because they light up. But what *doesn't* light up that they *don't* like?"

"Dentists?" suggested Mrs. Dooley.

"Homework?" said Sherman.

"Going to bed?" asked Wilmer.

"Paprika!" shouted Preston.

"Vegetables!" shouted Mr. Dooley. "All kids hate spinach. But imagine how many kids would love spinach if it glowed a sparkly orange!"

Wilmer wanted to point out that not all kids hated spinach, but decided not to voice the objection.

"So I invented . . ." Mr. Dooley paused for effect. "VeggiBUZZZZ!" He beamed with excitement. Then, dropping his voice to a deep, radio-announcer baritone, he continued, "Say good-bye to boring, dull-colored veggies. Kids will clamor for healthy food with new VeggiBUZZZZ! Dine on vegetables that not only glow, but are as sweet as sugar. With zero calories." He held out a plate of glowing purple carrots. Wilmer lifted one carefully with his pinky and thumb and studied it.

"It's completely safe," Mr. Dooley assured him.

Wilmer took a bite. He swallowed. Nothing happened. He was still the same regular-colored Wilmer.

But the carrot was wonderful! Carroty! Yet sweet—in a healthy, pure sort of way, Wilmer thought. It shone with a delicious, violet-hued glow. "Wow. That's really good."

"It's brilliant!" exclaimed Mrs. Dooley.

Wilmer nodded. "It really is, Dad."

Mrs. Dooley put Preston on the floor and gave her husband a big kiss on the cheek. "Well done, Ignatius. Well done!"

"Chili powder!" cried Preston.

"Not now, dear," said Mrs. Dooley.

"This invention took a long time to figure out," said Mr. Dooley. "The first few batches didn't do much at all. Getting the formula right took a lot of observation. In the end I just needed to add a few crucial ingredients, and the unusable batch was transformed into perfectly safe VeggiBUZZZZ! That's why I'm a great scientist. Observation!"

Wilmer looked at the still-blinking Sherman, who sat quietly and didn't mutter a word. "Don't you want to run around?" Wilmer asked.

"Not really," said Sherman.

"How do you feel?"

"Gassy," said Sherman.

Wilmer gulped.

Mrs. Dooley picked up Preston. "I think we should try that chili powder," she said, kissing her youngest son on his forehead. "Join us when you're done," she said to Mr. Dooley. "Just don't forget to wash your hands when you come up," she added, running a finger on his goggles and removing a streak of soot.

Mrs. Dooley carried Preston upstairs. Sherman slowly followed, barely making it past each step. Wilmer lingered behind, looking at his father's soot-smeared goggles.

Observation!

"That's it!" he shouted. "Dad? You don't have a sink down here."

"So?"

"You have to wash your hands upstairs every night. You bring up your jars for Mom to clean."

Mr. Dooley nodded. "Of course. Good science is clean science, I always say."

"A couple of weeks ago one of those dishes must have had some of the rejected VeggiBUZZZZ! solution in it," said Wilmer, waving his hands with excitement.

"Go on," said Mr. Dooley.

"Mom must have mistaken it for one of her pots—you know she does that all the time—and poured the VeggiBUZZZZ! water onto her garden. There it mixed with the turnip crop. She used the turnips in her muffin batter. I shared my muffins at school, but they were teeming with bacteria from the contaminated VeggiBUZZZZ! Kids ate them. And that's what created the Mumpley plague!" Wilmer took a deep breath. His hands were trembling he was so excited.

"Oh, Wilmer," said Mr. Dooley, his eyes watering.

"Don't cry, Dad," said Wilmer. "You didn't

know that would happen. It's not entirely your fault if hundreds of kids explode."

"I'm not crying because of that. I'm crying because I'm so proud. You're a Dooley, through and through!" He grasped Wilmer by his shoulders and smothered him in a big hug.

"Thanks, Dad," Wilmer said, choking. "Um, not so tight, please?"

"My son!" bellowed Mr. Dooley, squeezing him tighter. "You're an even better scientist than I was at your age!"

"Thanks. But, Dad, you're suffocating me, sort of," squawked Wilmer from within the folds of his father's arms. Still, it felt pretty good. "And we're not exactly out of the woods," he continued. His father released his grip. "We need to figure out a cure before Sherman explodes."

"Oh. Right," said Mr. Dooley. "But it can take months to find cures to diseases, son. Years!" Mr. Dooley scratched his head.

"You said you added a few ingredients to the bad batch of VeggiBUZZZZ! and that solved the problem. Stay here!"

III.

Wilmer dashed up the stairs two at a time. He imagined he was going even faster than Sherman ever ran. Two steps, two steps, up and up. On the first floor he raced past poor Sherman, who was lying on the couch, watching TV and barely moving.

Wilmer ran even faster. Up the stairs and to his room, and then back down. Finally, in the basement and panting, he held out his hand. On his palm lay two strands of pink hair. Roxie's hair.

"Put some of your perfected VeggiBUZZZZ! on these," said Wilmer.

"Really, Wilmer!" said Mr. Dooley. "Putting hair *into* food? What are you thinking? No one is going to buy VeggiBUZZZZ! as a shampoo. Although glowing shampoo isn't a horribly bad idea. Maybe for my next invention."

Wilmer shook his head, grabbed a small vial of formula, and poured a few drops on the vividly glowing pink hair. He leaned closer. He held his breath.

For a split second nothing happened.

But then, miraculously, the hair blinked. It sparkled. It turned into its natural, lustrous blond.

Wilmer exhaled and leaped into the air. "It worked!" he gasped, beaming with joy. "We've saved the school!"

"I'm not sure why you would want to shave the school," said Mr. Dooley. "Although that would be an interesting experiment. We could study the effects of hair growth and—"

"Not shave, SAVE!" cried Wilmer.

"That makes a lot more sense," agreed Mr. Dooley. "But we'll need to try this cure on a human subject. It will have to be someone we can test carefully. We'll have to track the disease over a series of days and tediously study the effect of the medicine. We can put an advertisement in a scientific journal and ask for volunteers."

"Or we can get Sherman. He's not looking very good."

"Yes. An ever better idea."

A few moments later Wilmer and his father shook Sherman from the couch.

"Sherman, we want you to eat something," said Wilmer.

"I'm not hungry, but thanks," said Sherman, smiling sleepily.

Not hungry! This was even worse than Wilmer had imagined!

"Quick! Eat this! Before you blow!" shouted Wilmer, holding a spoon near Sherman's lips.

Sherman shrugged and opened his mouth. Wilmer plunged the spoon inside.

Sherman swallowed.

Sherman burped.

Sherman jumped off the couch and immediately ran around the kitchen table in a respectable 5.1 seconds.

When he skidded to a halt, he was his normal color again.

Wilmer and his father hugged. "It works!" hollered Wilmer. "Dad, I'll need all the Veggi-BUZZZZ! you've got to share with the kids at school."

"We'll need to make a batch first," said Mr. Dooley. "We need to mash the components into powder and boil them in water. We should have just enough of my ingredients handy." Wilmer followed his father to the basement, narrowly avoiding Sherman, who was once again racing around the kitchen table and screaming, "Giddyup!" Wilmer had never been happier to be almost crashed into.

"I'm glad you came to me," said Mr. Dooley as they entered the lab. "Everyone needs help."

"Like you did. From Grandpa," said Wilmer, nodding. "You told me he helped you with your science project entry in sixth grade. But you never said how."

"So he did!" said Mr. Dooley. "As you may recall, I examined the effects that sugar had on slugs. I would never have come to my conclusion if your old gramps hadn't let me borrow his slug collection."

"Grandpa collected slugs?" said Wilmer with a mild tremble. Slugs were pretty disgusting.

"Why, yes. And leeches. He believed they had great healing powers when used to suck out blood. I always thought that somewhat unlikely."

"Good thinking, Dad."

His father began gathering ingredients. He

put a dozen items on the table but then peered into one of the top cabinets and frowned. He stood on his tiptoes to look closer and frowned again. He pulled out a small jar from the very, very back. It had only trace amounts of a fine dust. "We're low on cowitch powder. We can make enough cure for two doses, but that's about it. That's not nearly enough to save Mumpley."

"Doesn't cowitch powder just make you itch?" asked Wilmer, thinking back to his earlier experiments with the substance.

"Normally, yes. You have to be careful with it. Spill some on yourself, and you might itch so much you'll find yourself dancing a jig!" he said with a laugh.

"Don't worry, Dad," said Wilmer. "I know where they keep a fresh supply of cowitch at school." Mrs. Padgett wouldn't mind if he borrowed some.

"Excellent!" exclaimed Mr. Dooley. "You'll have to finish the cure at school. Do you have a lab you can work in?"

Wilmer nodded.

"Perfect. I'll write down the exact amount you

need." As Wilmer helped Mr. Dooley measure the rest of the ingredients, his mind raced, although not as quickly as Sherman was likely racing in circles upstairs.

He couldn't wait to get to school tomorrow and finally help his classmates. He would give the cure to Roxie first. No—he would give it to Ernie first. He needed to get his best friend back.

Tomorrow, he decided, he would also tell Roxie how he felt about her. Yes. He would give her the cure and declare his undying love.

Or maybe he would just give her the cure. He'd have to see about the declaring of love part.

"Dad, bring over that cowitch powder," said Wilmer. "I want to make a special supply of the Dooley Dose. For two."

MONDAY
Day 14

Dear Journal,

This morning Dad handed me a small container filled with powdered VeggiBUZZZZ! cure. We used up every necessary ingredient in his lab! Still, it's hard to believe this is enough for the entire town. We spent most of the night pulverizing them, squeezing them, mashing them, and measuring the precise amounts of everything the formula needed. Two microspoons of condensed beeswax. Three hundred yoctograms of herring. It was pain-staking work. The rest is up to me. I just need that cowitch powder (2.8 tablespoons) and a few quarts of water (4.693 quarts, to be exact) to complete the medicine.

We were up so late that I overslept. Dad drove me to school. He has a meeting today with the SugarBUZZZZ! company to unveil his new invention. But I think he was more excited about my discovery than he was his own. He wouldn't stop going on about how proud he is of me. Dad's convinced I'm a shoo-in for the Sixth-Grade Science Medal. But honestly, I just want to make sure no one explodes.

In addition to a small tub filled with powdered ingredients, I also have a small test tube filled with just enough ready-made antidote for two people. I can't wait to give it to Ernie and Roxie.

Soon they'll be cured. Everyone will be. It wasn't easy, but the best discoveries never are. That's why trial and error is so important. You have to have patience, to try things over and over and see what works.

I suppose that's true for romantic gestures, too. Maybe Roxie will be so impressed she'll swoon when she sees me.

I know just what I'll say to her. I'll look her in the eye, hold out my vial of VeggiBUZZZZ!, and say, "Hey, Roxie baby. I gots the cure. Yo!"

Okay. I won't say that. I won't try a British accent, either. I'll just wing it. You can experiment so much that you never get things done. Sometimes you just need to rush to trial. Sometimes you need to take a risk and see what happens, whether it's testing a spoonful of cure or wearing your heart on your sleeve.

Signing off,
Wilmer Dooley

I.

The powdered cure weighed only a few ounces, but it weighed on Wilmer's mind quite heavily. When he set foot into school that morning, his excitement ebbed and twisted into nervousness. What if Ernie wouldn't talk to him? What if Roxie ignored him? What if no one believed him?

What if it didn't work?

So instead of running around yelling that he had a cure, a real cure, Wilmer kept it hidden. Hopefully, no one would explode before he got up the nerve to share his discovery. He carried his backpack with him to class. He didn't want the Dooley Dose out of his sight.

Everyone in the sixth-grade wing had unmistakably slowed down over the weekend. They all shuffled at a snail's pace, as if everyone had aged seventy years—their backs hunched and their legs stiff.

Their colors were murky and gloomy too—they were covered in washes of rust and sienna, burnt orange and camouflage green. They grumbled and frowned. Their moods matched the dreariness of their hues.

In biology class Mrs. Padgett asked questions, but kids were too tired to raise their hands to answer them, except for Wilmer and Claudius. But then, they were the only two kids in school who were their normal colors. Their classmates eyed them with jealousy.

Mrs. Padgett called on Claudius for every easy question and asked Wilmer random, nearly impossible ones. But he knew all the answers. That seemed to annoy her.

"We are learning about what kind of forests? The words rhyme with 'brain forests.' Claudius?" asked Mrs. Padgett, pointing to her favorite student, his hand raised.

"Rain forests?" guessed Claudius.

"Excellent. And, Claudius, what sorts of animals might you find in the rain forest? One kind might rhyme with 'borilla' and another with 'balligator.'"

"Gorilla and alligator?" said Claudius.

"Very good, Mr. Dill. You are certainly a wonderful student. Three cheers for Mr. Dill! But let's give someone else a chance to answer a question. Wilmer, what is the melting point of calcium carbonate?"

Wilmer blinked. "Eight hundred twenty-five degrees Celsius. That's what eggshells are made from. But what does that have to do with the rain forest?"

"*I'll* ask the questions in this class, Wilmer Dooley! The last time I looked, I was still the teacher in this room. Unless you want to start teaching this class?"

Wilmer shrugged. "Okay."

"Never!" said Mrs. Padgett, aghast. "I should report you to the principal. That's called mutiny, Mr. Dooley! And I'm sure there are rules against it!"

Wilmer sighed and sat back.

Mrs. Padgett tapped her desk with a ruler.

Thwack, thwack, thwack. "Now, 'rain forest' starts with what letter of the alphabet? Claudius, do you know this one?"

"The letter *R*?" said Claudius.

"Excellent!" exclaimed Mrs. Padgett.

When class ended, kids tottered slowly down the hall as if they were senior citizens going to a shuffleboard tournament. Wilmer didn't like what he saw, not one bit. So he lingered behind, quickly unlocked the special science compartment in his backpack, and unzipped it. The small tub of Veggi-BUZZZZ! ingredients and the test tube filled with premade solution were both inside, safe and sound. It was time to save his friend, and the school. Ernie doddered out the door. Wilmer left his backpack on his seat and hurried after him.

"Hold up," he said, smiling.

"What do you want?" snapped Ernie, not stopping.

"I found a cure," said Wilmer. "For the epidemic." Wilmer kept his smile, but Ernie continued plodding away. Wilmer felt his smile begin to droop. "Didn't you hear me?"

"Yeah. Congratulations. I'm happy for you," said Ernie in a tone that implied quite the opposite.

"You should be," Wilmer barked back. He hated getting angry, but why was Ernie making it so hard? "I wanted you to have it first." Ernie didn't turn around; he just kept walking. "I'm talking to you!" shouted Wilmer. "I should make you apologize before I give you any!"

"Apologize?" screamed Ernie, stopping and turning in the hallway. "For what? You're the one that's been ignoring me. Why would I want your stupid cure, anyway?"

"Because if you don't take it, you'll explode."

"Maybe I want to explode!" yelled Ernie, although Wilmer doubted that was true. "*You* should apologize first."

"Me?" Wilmer snapped back. "You were practically the first kid in line to get the Claudius Cure. And you knew it *couldn't* be real. Don't you remember the lies he told about Copernicus? You were my friend! Are my friend. Were my friend. I don't know anymore."

Ernie narrowed his eyes as they stood in the hallway in front of his locker. Wilmer stared back. They both snorted from their noses, like two bulls. "I did *not* buy the Claudius Cure, okay? I wouldn't. I didn't. How could you think I'd trust Claudius?"

"But I saw you with a milk carton."

"Filled with milk! I like milk!" Wilmer hit his head with the palm of his hand. Of course! Ernie drank a carton every day. "I'm on your side. Don't you know that? And yes, I'm still your friend. Do you think something like this little fight would really end that?"

Wilmer looked down at the ground, his face flushing. "I guess not. Of course you wouldn't. I'm sorry, Ernie. I really am." Wilmer shook his head. "You must hate me."

"You're my best friend," said Ernie.

Wilmer looked away from his feet and at Ernie, who grinned. Wilmer grinned back. It felt great to find the cure, but it felt even better to have his best friend back. "I wanted you to be the first to have the cure. It works. I promise."

"If you say it works, of course it works," said Ernie. "You wouldn't say it if it wasn't true."

Ernie held up his thumb and Wilmer curled his thumb around it tightly. "I knew Claudius was a fraud from the start," said Ernie. "That's why we called the news station. To tell them about his cure being fake."

"That was you?" said Wilmer, surprised.

"Well, it was Roxie's idea." Ernie opened his locker. He removed a blue-glowing sock. "I found this in the boys' bathroom right after Claudius claimed to be cured. It's blue body paint. I think Claudius just painted himself and then washed it off. That's how his symptoms 'disappeared' so quickly."

Wilmer touched the now-crusty blue sock, amazed. "Why didn't you tell me?"

"I tried to, but you wouldn't listen. I kept the sock here for a few days, until I finally showed it to Roxie. She told me you'd discovered that the Claudius Cure was just a bunch of sugar water. You and Claudius are the only two kids in school who stay away from SugarBUZZZZ! He's allergic. And you're just weird. No offense."

"Spinach is healthier for you," said Wilmer. "It contains folate and manganese to improve brain function."

"I know," said Ernie. "You've told me. Anyway, Roxie and I called Gwendolyn Bray."

Wilmer put his hand on Ernie's shoulder. His eyes misted, but he wiped the moisture away quickly. "I'm sorry I ever doubted you, Ernie. Now let's get you and everyone else cured."

Ernie held out his hand. "Let's have it. I'm ready."

"It's in my backpack."

His backpack!

He had left it in Mrs. Padgett's class, on his seat. He rushed down the hall. For a moment his heart hiccupped. What if someone had taken his unguarded backpack? How could he have just left it there?

Wilmer ran inside the now-empty classroom. He took a deep breath of relief. His backpack was exactly where he'd left it. He had been worried for no reason. Wilmer grabbed the strap and took a step forward. As he did, a pair of rubber gloves fell out of his special science compartment. In his rush to catch Ernie he had left the pocket unzipped! He bent down to pick up the gloves. But as he stuffed them back into the compartment, his eyes bulged and his hands shook.

The Dooley Dose. It was gone.

II.

Wilmer Dooley. Wilmer Dooley. Wilmer Dooley. Seldom had two words created as much hatred as that which now stirred in Claudius Dill's head. All morning kids had been demanding refunds for his Claudius Cure, and many more threw him accusatory looks, as if he had created a phony cure on purpose. Well, maybe he had! So? He would have gotten away with it if not for Wilmer Dooley. Wilmer Dooley. Wilmer Dooley.

Claudius was convinced it was Wilmer Dooley who had tattled on him to the news station. Who else would have done it? Wilmer Dooley was responsible for everybody talking about Claudius behind his back! For shunning him! For no longer asking for autographs!

Claudius couldn't look at Wilmer, since

Wilmer sat behind him in the last row, but he could sense him there, and his hatred sizzled like light rain on burning coals. When class ended, Wilmer rushed out of the room, but Claudius held back, staring after him with eyes that, if they had laser beams, would have burned through Wilmer's skull, bounced off the wall, and burned through it again. Claudius thought about chasing him out the door, jumping on his back, and hitting him with his schoolbooks. But Claudius was not violent. He was a liar and a cheat and an evil genius, but violent? Never.

But wait—this was interesting. Wilmer had left his backpack behind. There it was, on his chair. Was it an accident? Or a ruse? Maybe Wilmer wanted Claudius to snoop through his things. Maybe Wilmer hoped Claudius would peek into his notebook.

Well, Claudius wouldn't let him down.

Claudius scanned the room. Empty. Even Mrs. Padgett had left. Claudius marched to Wilmer's desk. He knew that Wilmer kept his science compartment locked. Twice before Claudius had tried to sneak a peek into Wilmer's backpack pocket contents but had been unsuccessful. So this time when Claudius checked the chamber, he expected to be thwarted again.

But when he reached Wilmer's chair, Claudius trembled with excitement. The lock was off. The compartment was unzipped!

Claudius peered inside. He saw rubber gloves. Boring. He sifted past empty test tubes. Also boring. But at the bottom of the pocket was a clear plastic tub filled with glowing green powder, and a small test tube filled with a liquid of the exact same color. Both shared identical labels: THE DOOLEY DOSE.

The Dooley Dose? Had he done it? Had Wilmer actually found a cure? Claudius's brain filled with a picture of a smiling, famous Wilmer waving to crowds on a parade float. The thought made Claudius sick. He could never let that happen! Scowling, Claudius swiped the test tube out of the backpack and plunged it into his back pocket. He cradled the plastic tub in his hands and stuck it under his shirt.

Now let Wilmer try to take credit for curing

the epidemic. It would be pretty hard without his precious Dooley Dose. Smiling, and even stifling a wicked laugh, Claudius hurried from the room.

Maybe Claudius could take credit for this exciting discovery. A brand-new and improved Claudius Cure! At last his father, the famous Dr. Dill, would be proud of his son's scientific brilliance.

III.

Mrs. Padgett halted before she entered her classroom. She had rushed out to grab a cup of coffee but hurried back after remembering she didn't drink coffee. By chance, she peered through the small window before pushing open the door, and spied Claudius Dill. He was looking through his backpack. No, not his. Wilmer's. That was Wilmer's desk, no doubt about it: There were burn marks on the edges from a lab explosion. What was Claudius up to? She should run in there right now. She should tell that boy not to look through things that weren't his own. She should report him to the principal at once!

But this was Claudius Dill. Behind him, her

whiteboards sparkled. And that wasn't any kid's backpack—it was Wilmer Dooley's. So Mrs. Padgett did not do any of the things she should have done; instead she watched Claudius put a small test tube into his pocket and a tub of plasticware under his shirt.

Stealing! That was even worse than sneaking. But if it was good for Claudius, it was no doubt bad for Wilmer. So she stayed in the shadows, and when she saw Claudius hurry toward the door, she stepped back quietly so he would not see her.

IV.

"It's gone," Wilmer yowled, holding up his backpack and peering inside. "Someone has taken the Dooley Dose! I left it unguarded for only a minute!"

"Just make some more," suggested Ernie.

"I can't! Dad and I used up all the ingredients!"

"Then we'll wait a few days," Ernie said, and yawned.

"You don't understand. If people don't take this cure soon, they'll explode!"

"I thought you were kidding about that earlier."

"Nope. I wish I were."

Ernie frowned. Wilmer didn't like the idea of his best friend exploding, but he assumed Ernie liked the idea even less. Then Wilmer noticed a note on the ground next to his foot. "Someone must have left this behind," he said. He bent down to pick it up.

He and Ernie read it together. There were just four words on it, handwritten in a messy, quickly scribbled scrawl: "You'll never win, Dooley."

Wilmer stared, openmouthed. "I think that's Claudius's handwriting."

Ernie nodded. "He's the only guy I know who puts hearts over his *i*'s instead of dots."

"Which really isn't very fitting for this type of note," Wilmer added.

"I bet he's going to take the credit for your cure," said Ernie, snapping his fingers. "Just like with Copernicus! We have to find Claudius and make him give it back."

"How?" sighed Wilmer, shaking his head. "I'm not going to fight him. I'm not the strong type." He sighed again. "Or the silent type, I guess. But I do a nice British accent."

"We should tell a teacher. We should tell the school."

"And why would they believe me?" Wilmer groaned, frowning. "I tried to tell everyone the Claudius Cure was fake, but no one listened. I've always said Claudius didn't cure Copernicus, but no one believes that, either. Why would anyone listen to me now?"

"Because you have me on your side," said Ernie, holding his thumb up. Wilmer wrapped it with his, but it didn't cheer him up. "We'll convince the school together." Ernie broke into a grin. "And I know exactly what we can do. C'mon!"

Wilmer followed Ernie as he hurried down the hall, although Ernie's idea of hurrying was shuffling slowly.

"Do you feel gassy?" asked Wilmer. Ernie nodded. Wilmer gulped.

"Roxie!" said Ernie, waving. She stood by her locker, removing her book bag for class. She looked up. "We need your help!"

V.

Wilmer sat in Mrs. Hawthorne's English class, checking the clock every two minutes, counting down until 11:25. That was exactly five minutes before lunchtime, when the *Monday Mumpley Musings* radio show began. Every other week Roxie McGhee broadcast a musing—some keen observation or investigative report about school. Previous topics had included mystery meat in the cafeteria (what sort of meat was it, and was it even meat?), the sorry state of school-supplied swimsuits, and "How Old Is That Gum Under Your Desk? An Exposé!"

During the broadcasts, as Roxie's voice trickled through the room, Wilmer liked to close his eyes and pretend she was speaking to him, and to him alone.

This morning Claudius sat in his chair, up one row and over. He occasionally glanced back at Wilmer with a look of unbridled hatred. Wilmer tried not to return the stare. He knew Claudius would get what was coming to him very soon.

As Mrs. Hawthorne prattled on about prepositions, Wilmer glanced at the clock to see if the seconds were going a few zeptoseconds slower, per his earlier thesis. He thought they were, but the difference was difficult to pinpoint without a more finely tuned measuring instrument.

Finally the loudspeaker threw out a long squeal. Even though he was waiting for it, the shrill voice of Principal Shropshire shocked Wilmer. It squawked through the static. "Excuse me, um, classes. Welcome to our biweekly Monday radio show, *Monday Mumpley Musings*, with our star reporter, Roxie McGhee. Not that she's an actual star, like in the astronomical sense. Not saying that. No, she's a student here and . . ."

A few more crackles rang out, followed by some thuds and rattling noises, as if the microphone was being ripped from someone's hands. "Ow, hey!" said the principal, and then following another thump, Roxie spoke, like an angel from the skies. "Thank you, Principal Shropshire. This is Roxie McGhee of *Mumpley Musings*. Today's musing is titled 'The Mumpley Plague: Fact and Fiction.'

"We all know the facts. A strange disease.

Unlimited energy. And now a crash. A sugar crash, it turns out.

"Like many of you, I was excited about this colorful contagion at first. It was fun to be pink. Even though my nose was stuffed and my throat was a little sore, it was worth it, just for something a little different.

"Like how Halloween is fun while you're wearing a costume. But it's nice to know you can take that costume off whenever you want and go back to being yourself.

"But we couldn't take off our colors. And soon we realized that being colorful wasn't really very special. Because it's not what we are on the outside that's important. It's what's on the inside. It's not our colors. It's things like honesty and being a good friend. Those are the most important things."

Wilmer and Ernie exchanged looks as Roxie spoke. They kept smiling as she told the school everything. Roxie recounted how Ernie had found Claudius's paint-smeared sock. How Claudius had only pretended to be sick. How the cure was fake.

In class a few kids muttered under their

breath. Many looked over to Claudius and snarled. Claudius cringed and slumped in his seat, but not before throwing Wilmer a look of utter loathing.

And then Roxie told the school how Wilmer had found a cure, and all he needed to do was add one final ingredient.

"But, Claudius, it's not too late!" she pleaded. "You don't have to continue this charade. If it's what's inside that counts, show us what's inside of you. I know there is good in there. We all make mistakes. Give the cure back to Wilmer. Let him put a stop to the Mumpley malady.

"This is Roxie McGhee. And that's nothing but the truth!"

The loudspeaker squealed and the jarring voice of Principal Shropshire came back over the PA system. "Will Claudius Dill report to the principal's office at once," he snapped, and then the speaker went silent.

All eyes hovered on Claudius as he stood up, grabbed his books, and strode toward the door. He stopped just long enough to lean over to Wilmer and growl in a voice only Wilmer could

hear, "Meet me behind the bleachers after class."

Claudius exited the room. The students took a collective breath. And then Zane Bradley stood up. His dull pea green face flashed with muted umber trapezoids. He smiled, and shouted, "Three cheers for Wilmer Dooley!"

Maybe Zane wasn't as much of an ignoramus as Wilmer thought.

The entire class burst into cheers as Wilmer blushed. Ernie's wolf whistles were the loudest of them all.

VI.

Wilmer skipped lunch and instead headed out toward the bleachers. At first he didn't see anyone. But when he took a few more steps, he found Claudius sitting on the ground, underneath the seats, away from view. His enemy held the plastic tub of Dooley Dose ingredients, lobbing it lightly from palm to palm. When he saw Wilmer, he tossed it to him.

"Take it. Just take it," he barked. "Everyone hates me now, anyway, because of you. You must be happy. You won. You're just lucky my dad isn't here.

He would have put you in your place. He would have found a cure way before you. It's not his fault he's so busy. But I'll show him. And you. And everyone. Soon!"

Wilmer held the canister tightly in his hand. He needed to prepare the ingredients immediately so that he could share the cure with the rest of the school. But as he started to leave, he hesitated. He looked down at Claudius, who was staring unhappily at the ground. Although Wilmer hated Claudius more than puppies hate kittens, he couldn't help but think about what Claudius had said.

Wilmer knew what it was like to try to make a father proud. He knew how it felt to be constantly trying to live up to big expectations, and not always succeeding. Wilmer thought of his father's mantel filled with awards. As bad as Wilmer felt sometimes about the need to make his own mark, maybe Claudius had it worse. Maybe they weren't that different from each other.

"You know," said Wilmer. "Everyone is going to need this cure. There's still some work I need to do. I could use a hand."

"You could?" asked Claudius, beading his eyes in distrust. "So?"

"Want to help?"

Claudius's eyes lit up for a moment but then dimmed. He paused and croaked, "Really?"

"Come on. The Dooley Dose could use a little Claudius Convincing."

Claudius stood up and removed a glowing green test tube from his back pocket. "Here. This is yours too."

VII.

Wilmer found Ernie in the lunchroom and gave him half of the premade Dooley Dose. Ernie coughed twice. His dull green face blinked three times. And then the color simply vanished. Ernie looked in surprise at his arm, now back to its normal color.

"How do you feel?" asked Wilmer.

"Colorless," said Ernie. "And not gassy at all."

Next Wilmer and Ernie found Roxie by her locker with Vonda and Claire. When they saw Wilmer, Roxie's friends didn't look happy.

"I still don't trust you," sneered Vonda to Wilmer. "Not in the least." She and Claire turned and started to walk away. "Are you coming?" she barked as Roxie paused.

"Wait," said Wilmer. He sucked in a breath. He held out the half-full test tube to Roxie. "It's the Dooley Dose. I wanted you to be the first to have it. Actually, that's not right. You'll be the third. After Ernie and my brother."

Roxie looked at the formula, sniffed it, and paused. "What's in it?"

"Trust me," said Wilmer.

"You're not trusting *him*, are you?" spat Vonda.

"Yes, I am," Roxie said, and downed the vial in one gulp. Her pink wiped away like a strong wave. She gasped. Vonda and Claire gasped too.

Shuffling students still crammed the hall-way. Even the octogenarian algebra teacher, Mrs. Mohair, sped past most of them, cane in hand. The slowly crawling kids barely had the energy to reach their lockers. "We better make more," Wilmer said. "Or this whole school will blow."

Roxie scuffled off with her friends. Where was she going now? But Wilmer couldn't worry about it. He and Ernie headed to the science lab. As they neared it, the PA system crackled.

"The cure has been recovered. Please make your way to the science lab for your *free* Dooley Dose," said Vonda.

Cheers echoed through the school. Ernie and Wilmer met Claudius outside the lab. Standing next to him was an eggplant-flashing Ronny Roswick, stooped over and barely moving.

"I found him lying in the middle of the hall," said Claudius. "He doesn't have much time left."

"I feel gassy." Ronny moaned.

"Then let's make that cure!" shouted Wilmer, pushing open the door.

Mrs. Padgett stood in the way, arms crossed, still as a statue.

"Where do you think *you're* going?" she growled.

"Didn't you hear?" said Wilmer. "We need to prepare batches to save everyone. We have all the ingredients." He held out the plastic tub. "Well, most of them. We need some cowitch powder."

Mrs. Padgett shook her head and stood her ground. "I'll have you know, Mr. Dooley," she said, spittle flying out of her mouth as she angrily growled each syllable, "that this is *my* science lab. This is *my* equipment. Students are not allowed in here without *my* permission. And they are certainly not allowed to touch my precious supply of cowitch!"

"But we have to!" Wilmer shouted anxiously.

"Ronny's going to explode," said Ernie, pointing to Ronny Roswick. Ronny's stomach was expanding at an alarming speed.

"That's not my concern," snapped Mrs. Padgett. "*My* concern is missing test tubes. A stolen microscope. Vanishing cowitch. And you"— she jabbed her long, crooked finger at Wilmer— "are guilty! Oh, maybe not by a jury, or even by the foolish Principal Shropshire. But guilty all the same."

Wilmer wanted to shake her and scream that they needed to use her equipment and cowitch *now*! That he couldn't make a difference without it! That he wasn't sorry he'd used her stuff and that he would never stop, whether she wanted him to or not.

But science wasn't only about making discoveries, he reminded himself. It was about convincing, too. Science was about people as much as it was about chemicals. So he swallowed his frustration and bowed his head. "I'm sorry. You're right. I should have asked permission. Mrs. Padgett, can we please use your equipment and cowitch powder to save the school and keep Ronny Roswick from blowing up all over the room?"

Mrs. Padgett stood firm, her arms still crossed. "Absolutely not."

Claudius stepped forward. "Mrs. Padgett, you have to."

"*Et tu,* Claudius?" Mrs. Padgett hissed. "I'm surprised to see you helping *him.*" When she said "him," her lips curled in disgust and she pointed to Wilmer. "I expected more from you, Claudius."

"Wilmer is right. We need to use the lab. If you don't let us, I'll never clean your whiteboards again!" Claudius barked.

"What?" said Mrs. Padgett, stepping back.

"I've been sucking up to you all year, and I won't do it anymore," said Claudius, jabbing his finger forward. "Now let us in. We're going to make that formula. Now!"

Mrs. Padgett's face twisted in shock. She looked over at her whiteboard, which was filled with scientific diagrams from class and needed to be cleaned. Surely, no one could expect *her* to clean it! She looked at Claudius, then at Ernie and Wilmer. Finally she looked at Ronny Roswick, whose stomach was now the shape of a large cantaloupe.

She stepped aside. "Do as you must," she sighed.

VIII.

With cylinders, burners, and all the other lab equipment finally at their disposal, Claudius and Wilmer were in business. They quickly mixed 2.8 tablespoons of cowitch into Wilmer's tub of carefully measured ingredients and poured them into a pot filled with exactly 4.693 quarts of distilled water. They placed it over a Bunsen burner. Ronny Roswick's stomach now looked quite like that of a small whale. It made strange gurgling noises, like an excited hot tub.

"Hurry!" shouted Ernie. Claudius dipped a spoon into the pot and plunged the cure into Ronny's open mouth.

Within seconds of taking the Dooley Dose, Ronny's purple vanished, his stomach shrank, and he skipped out of the room whistling.

Although the school day was not officially over, classrooms emptied. A long line of kids quickly stretched out from the lab. But the teachers didn't mind. In fact, a few of them were in line too.

"Is it really made out of *vegetables*?" asked Mason Allbright, holding a spoonful of cure up to his mustard-and-sepia–striped face.

"Just take it!" hollered Carly Trundle from behind. Her dull liver-toned skin reminded Wilmer of a zombie.

Mason shrugged, winced, and swallowed his dose. His natural color returned instantly and he licked his lips. "Hey. Not bad. I guess veggies aren't so horrible after all." He leaned over to Wilmer. "Don't you dare tell my parents I said that."

As Wilmer, Ernie, and Claudius continued dispensing the cure, Gwendolyn Bray spoke only a few feet away, surrounded by a small camera crew.

"It appears the Dooley Dose, invented by Mumpley Middle School's Wilmer Dooley, is 100 percent effective. As we speak, busloads of sick kids from neighboring schools are being dropped off to get in line, and the parking lot is filling up with people from around town who caught the contagion. It seems it will be a long afternoon here at Mumpley. But Wilmer Dooley, with the help of Claudius Dill and Ernie Rinehart, has saved the day."

Next to Gwendolyn Bray stood Mrs. Padgett, fluffing her hair. "They are making it with *my* science equipment and my precious supply of cowitch," she said, leaning into the microphone. "Mine. Valveeta Padgett. With two *t*'s."

"So you're a hero too. It must be an honor having Wilmer Dooley as a student," said Gwendolyn

Bray, holding her microphone up to the biology teacher's mouth.

Mrs. Padgett winced but then looked into the camera and smiled. "Oh, yes. He's always been my favorite."

Principal Shropshire stood next to Wilmer. They watched as Ernie and Claudius handed out spoonfuls of cure to eager students. "Nicely done," said the principal. "You'll make a fine dentist."

There was a bit of commotion at the lab door as a couple of people tried to squeeze their way past the line of kids. Then someone shouted, "That's Mr. Dooley. Let him through!" The line parted, and Mr. and Mrs. Dooley entered the room. Mr. Dooley held a large box. They saw Wilmer and hurried up to him.

"You have some boy there," said Principal Shropshire to Mr. and Mrs. Dooley, patting Wilmer on the head.

"I know," said Mrs. Dooley, beaming.

"So," said Mr. Dooley quietly, whispering in the principal's ear, but loud enough that Wilmer could hear, "do you think Wilmer will win the Sixth-Grade Science Medal for this?"

"It's not my decision," said Principal Shropshire. "It's hers." He pointed to Mrs. Padgett, who fluffed her hair and posed as news reporters snapped her picture. "But I suppose Wilmer has a pretty good chance, don't you?"

Gwendolyn Bray sped over. So did her camera crew. "Mr. Dooley. Is it true you were the cause of all this?" She shoved her microphone at his face.

Mr. Dooley nodded. "I'm afraid so." He cleared his throat, and when he spoke, his voice boomed across the room. He held up his large box. "But I've brought free samples of my new invention, VeggiBUZZZZ!, here for everyone. I know it won't make up for everything that's happened, but I hope everyone likes it." He removed small, ketchup-size packets from the box. "Veggi-BUZZZZ! makes vegetables taste like candy. One hundred percent healthy. And I guarantee there are no side effects!"

All the kids in the room cheered, although the parents and teachers in the room cheered even louder. Those who were already cured ran up for free samples.

"Looks like you've got a hit there, Dad," said Wilmer.

"Looks like we both do. Like father, like son," said Mr. Dooley.

Wilmer didn't stop smiling for a week.

THREE WEEKS LATER

Dear Journal,

I haven't written in this journal for quite some time. I've been too busy. I appeared on television with Gwendolyn Bray twice. I've been interviewed for six magazines, including two science journals. I can't walk down the hall without people asking to shake my hand. Even Mrs. Padgett has been nice to me. She says I can use her lab anytime I want, although I can't touch her precious cowitch powder again, no matter what. I returned her microscope and twelve of her fourteen test tubes the other day. She said I could keep the other two. After all, a scientist needs test tubes.

I've been busy catching up on my homework, especially my history project. Epidemics, like those in the Middle Ages, are frightening. They spread quickly and can be very destructive. But one thing is crucial no matter what year it is—the Power of Observation!

In fact, that's what eventually got rid of the Black Plague. People observed that when they kept their homes clean and rat-free, people stopped getting sick.

I got my paper back yesterday. An A+! Mr. Havendash said it was the best history report he had ever read in school. Dad was so proud of me when I showed it to him. And Mom let me decide what we were having for dinner that night.

She was a bit disappointed when I suggested spinach salads. But making an avocado and lime-roasted marshmallow dressing improved her spirits. Preston suggested she add the squeeze of lime juice, and I have to admit that it was a good idea.

I also officially handed in a report on the Mumpley plague and the Dooley Dose for my Sixth-Grade Science Medal entry. I wanted to include some samples, like Ernie's green-smeared tissues, but Mrs. Padgett didn't let me; she said they were disgusting. But I did include photographs, and a vial of the cure itself.

Tonight is the sixth-grade graduation ceremony, so I'll find out if I won. I haven't talked to Roxie since I gave her the cure. I almost talked to her three and a half times since then, but Vonda and Claire were always next to her, and I lost my nerve. Besides, I've seen her walking with Zane Bradley again. Ernie says they aren't dating, but I don't know. With summer vacation starting tomorrow, today's probably the last day I'll see her until school next year. Which means I'll have three months to get up the nerve to talk to her again.

I know science discoveries don't happen by themselves; you need to observe and experiment and see what happens. I suppose I should talk to Roxie today and see what happens too. But it's a lot easier to experiment on a sample of glowing green snot than the most glorious girl at Mumpley Middle School.

Signing off,
Wilmer Dooley

During the sixth-grade awards Wilmer sat sandwiched between his mom and dad. Sherman and

Preston were home with the babysitter, old Mrs. Brumbles from down the street. As Wilmer and his parents left, Sherman had raced around the kitchen table as usual. Mrs. Brumbles had tried to catch him and already looked exhausted after a minute. Mrs. Dooley had promised her they'd be home early. The babysitter looked relieved to hear it.

All the sixth graders and their parents were in the auditorium for the awards. Ernie sat directly behind Wilmer and kept kicking his chair. It was funny the first three times, but by the forty-second chair kicking Wilmer wanted to turn around and box his friend's ears.

Claudius was in the audience too. Wilmer noticed that Dr. Dill was not. Claudius and Wilmer locked eyes, but they didn't smile at each other. They may have banded together to save the school, but that didn't mean they were friends.

A few awards were given out first. The Foreign Language Award was handed to Gabi Lersh, who gave her acceptance speech in German, French, and Swedish. The Physical Fitness Award was given to Zane Bradley. He flashed a big smile to Roxie, but she returned it halfheartedly, giving Wilmer hope that maybe Ernie was right about them.

The English Award was given to "our star reporter, Roxie McGhee." Wilmer clapped so hard his palms hurt. She thanked the faculty, and as she walked back to her seat, her eyes met Wilmer's. Wilmer blushed. Roxie blushed too. Wilmer was relieved to see that she blushed a very healthy and very normal color.

Finally it was time for the science award. Mrs. Padgett made her way to the front of the stage from her seat with the other senior teaching staff. Her very high heels made her even taller than she was normally. She stared at the crowd, her eyes burrowing down at them. A few parents shifted uncomfortably. Mrs. Padgett had a way of intimidating practically anyone.

"The last few weeks have been trying times for Mumpley Middle School," she said, her husky voice scratching over the crowd like a wool coat. "Trying times indeed. We know about the contagion that tried us all. And we are aware of the efforts of some to rectify it. I won't mention names, but the cure was cooked in my science lab. I'm sure you've all seen my five-page profile in *Mumpley Life* magazine and my new column on online mah-jongg."

A number of people in the audience murmured that they had.

"But that's neither here nor there. I can't win the award, after all. Apparently, there are rules against that sort of thing, as Principal Shropshire has told me repeatedly."

From his seat at the back of the stage Principal Shropshire nodded.

"So that brings us here," continued Mrs. Padgett. "The prestigious Sixth-Grade Science Medal is a tradition that goes back some forty years and has been won by an impressive list of luminaries. Some of our brightest students have stood on this very stage to accept this esteemed prize.

"But, as I said, this year has proven to be quite trying, and a remarkable achievement deserves a remarkable award winner."

Ernie kicked Wilmer's chair, harder. This was it. Wilmer wondered if he should begin walking to the aisle now to accept his trophy, or stay in his seat until his name was announced. He chose to remain seated.

"But science is a funny thing. It takes many fortuitous events for great theories to bud, like photosynthesized flowers. It takes many people, too—some not always appropriately saluted. Sir Isaac Newton may have thought of gravity when an apple fell, but what of the farmer that grew the apple? The workers who fertilized it? The apple picker who should have removed the apple the day before but didn't bother because he was too lazy? Shouldn't they share the accolades as much as this Newton fellow, or even more so, since all he did was sit in the shade? Is that our idea of science?

"I say no!

"It is not just the person who observes. It is those who inspire him." Mrs. Padgett looked at Roxie. "It is those who stand by their friends even when they are treated unfairly." She stared at Ernie. "It is those who ignore grievances in the name of helping others." She sneaked a peek at Claudius. Then she scanned the entire crowd. "And it is those who freely volunteer samples for testing, and face illness and the threat of explosion, without asking for recognition in return."

Wilmer shifted uneasily. If she was giving him the award, it was an odd speech.

"No. It is everyone here that deserves to be acknowledged. That is why this year's Sixth-Grade Science Medal goes to the entire sixth-grade class."

From his seat at the back of the stage Principal Shropshire shouted, "Hooray for the courageous kids of Mumpley Middle School!"

A surprised roar rang out across the room. Parents shouted in unison, "Hooray for the courageous kids! Hooray for the courageous kids!" The entire sixth-grade class stood up and began filing toward the stage to pose for a picture.

Wilmer joined the crowd in the aisle just as Claudius Dill walked past. Claudius sneered. "I'm going to win the Seventh-Grade Science Medal next year by myself," he spat.

"We'll see," Wilmer shot back.

On the stage with the entire class posing for

their picture, Wilmer stood next to Roxie. On the other side of the group, Claudius stood next to Vonda Binkowski. Wilmer couldn't be sure, but he thought he saw Vonda throw Claudius a wink. Next to them, Ernie stood next to Claire. Ernie was singing to her while blowing his nose, but she refused to look at him.

"Congratulations on your prize," Wilmer said to Roxie after the picture was snapped.

"Congratulations on yours," said Roxie.

"Me? I didn't win anything."

"Well, you should have," she said. She bent over and kissed Wilmer on the cheek. "I hope I see you this summer. Call me!" Before Wilmer could say anything, she ran away to join Claire and Vonda down the stage steps.

As Wilmer stood in shock, Ernie came up to him. He slapped Wilmer's back. "I can't believe you didn't win that medal," he said. "A total rip-off."

"I don't know," said Wilmer, feeling his cheek with his hand. "Everything seems pretty great to me."

The ceremony had ended. As the Dooleys rose from their chairs to leave, Mr. Dooley wrapped his arms around Wilmer with a tight hug. "Have I told you how proud I am of you?"

"Proud? But I didn't win the Sixth-Grade Science Medal," said a surprised Wilmer.

"Sure you did. Along with two hundred other kids."

"That's not the same thing."

"Why not? In my eyes you won the science medal. If other kids won too, well, then their parents should be proud as well," said Mr. Dooley.

Wilmer spied Claudius walking out with Mrs. Dill. He wondered if Dr. Dill would be as proud of Claudius as Mr. Dooley was of Wilmer. He wondered if Dr. Dill would even notice.

"Dad, can I ask you something?" said Wilmer.

"Of course, son," said Mr. Dooley.

"You know I admire you, right? You're the greatest scientist I know."

"You're a great scientist too."

"Thanks. But really. You are. But . . . would you be mad if I didn't become a scientist like you?"

Mr. Dooley stopped and stared into Wilmer's

eyes. He seemed wounded by Wilmer's words. "What else would you be?"

"Working with the Dooley Dose made me realize something. I think I can do more good as a doctor."

"I've always wanted a doctor in the family," said Mrs. Dooley, who stood behind them.

"Funny. Me too," said Mr. Dooley. "Now let's hurry home before Mrs. Brumbles has a heart attack from running around the kitchen table trying to keep up with Sherman."

Tuesday
Day 1

Dear Journal,

   I'm starting this notebook (on official scientific graph paper!) to record my attempts at winning the affections of Roxie McGhee, the most beautiful and glorious girl in school. Her blond hair shines like a million SugarBUZZZZ!-inspired fireflies!

   That was a joke. Fireflies inspired my dad to create his famous invention. I'll have to write that story down when I get a chance. I've only heard it 216 times.

   That's an accurate number, by the way. I've counted.

   If my efforts go awry, I might also write down any scientific observations I have. After all, a scientist always observes! We'll see how it goes.

   I've done research on the best ways to attract a female:

- Peacocks display their feathers and then perform a weird courtship dance. If Roxie saw me dance, I'm pretty sure she'd start laughing and never stop. And I don't have feathers. So scratch that idea.
- Penguins sing, but I may very well be an even worse singer than I am a dancer.
- Porcupines pee on their mates to show they like them. I can't see that working on Roxie, though. I'm quite sure she'd never talk to me again.

So maybe the animal kingdom is a lousy place to look for ideas.

However, I have a hypothesis that gifts often win a woman's heart. More specifically, sharing the contents of one's lunch box will gain favor with the test subject, who in this case is Roxie McGhee.

Mom gave me a sarsaparilla turnip muffin in my lunch box today. It would be way too sweet for my taste, but it does have a pretty glow about it. It is the perfect present to offer Roxie. Hopefully, I can figure out a way to sit at the same lunch table as her so that I can attempt my romantic gesture.

Who knows? This time tomorrow she might be tickled pink to talk to me!

Signing off,
Wilmer Dooley

ACKNOWLEDGMENTS

I would like to acknowledge those presidents whose mustaches I most admire. In no particular order: William Howard Taft, Chester A. Arthur, Theodore Roosevelt, and Grover Cleveland.

I would also like to acknowledge, but less so than the presidents I just mentioned, the little people who have helped me rise to the top echelon of fiction writing excellence. I forget their names. I think one of them is named John something-something.

Lastly, my eternal gratitude to my editor, Emma Ledbetter, without whom this tome would not exist, and to those at Simon & Schuster whom I will forever lovingly refer to as "those at Simon & Schuster." I also tip my fedora—the green one—to the team at New Leaf Literary & Media, including the esteemed Joanna Volpe and Danielle Barthel, to whom I beg forgiveness for the unfortunate turkey sandwich incident.

—F. D.